ALEX SHEARER

SCHOLASTIC INC.
New York Toronto London Auckland Sydney
Mexico City New Delhi Hong Kong Buenos Aires

ISBN-13: 978-0-545-12107-1
ISBN-10: 0-545-12107-8

Text copyright © 2006 by Alex Shearer. All rights reserved. Published by Scholastic Inc. by agreement with Macmillan Children's Books, a division of Macmillan Publishing Limited, London, England. SCHOLASTIC and associated logos are trademarks and/or registered trademarks of Scholastic Inc.

12 11 10 9 8 7 6 5 4 3 2   9 10 11 12 13/0

Printed in the U.S.A.   40

This edition first printing, November 2008

Book design by Phil Falco

PART 1

Diary of F. Bamfield.

My room, my house, my street, my town, England, Europe, the world, the universe. (Wherever that is.)

Month of March.

Private.

No unauthorized persons to read this.

If you are reading this and you are not F. Bamfield, then you are an unauthorized person

So stop reading now.

Or you'll be in your coffin.

March 15

Dear Diary,

I'm not filling you in every day as I can't be bothered. Just now and again. In fact, this is my first entry since January, as you will know, being a diary. I'm only writing today because I had one of those weird dreams again.

I woke up during the night and I could have sworn that the walls were all silver and made out of metal, like stainless steel or something like that.

I thought for a minute that I had turned into a sardine.

But, fortunately, I hadn't.

I don't know what to make of my dreams sometimes.

I think I might need to see a ~~sighcoal~~ . . . a ~~psicyel~~ . . . a ~~sickoologist~~ . . . one of those brain doctors who looks at your head.

Anyway, that's it for news, more or less.

I have a pretty boring life really.

Nothing exciting ever happens to me.

1. TAKE A GAMBLE

It could have been stamps. It could have been stickers, or post-cards, or model airplanes, or the free gifts in cereal boxes. It could have been pictures of soccer players. It might even have been fossils, or film posters, or bargains from eBay. It could have been science-fiction stuff. It could have been coins. It could have been autographs of famous people. But it wasn't.

It was tin cans.

And the only explanation for them seemed to be that Fergal Bamfield was clever.

***

Fergal Bamfield found his reputation for cleverness as irritating as it was undeserved. It weighed heavily upon him, like a bag full of bricks.

It wasn't that he was stupid; far from it. He was capable and got good — often above average — marks in his exams. It was his eccentric appearance that marked him out. His unruly hair stuck out at all angles and could never be tamed, not even with a pot of gel. And then there were his glasses, which not only enlarged his eyes, but somehow had the effect of making his very head (and by implication his brain) seem bigger than it really was. The overall effect was that of "the mad professor's apprentice." (Or perhaps "the professor's mad apprentice" might have been a bit more accurate.)

The general rule seemed to be that he who looks like an eccentric genius must be an eccentric genius. Appearance was destiny. So Fergal came to acquire a reputation for extreme cleverness, which he hated. He hated it because he knew he didn't deserve it and he hated it because he felt pressured to live up to it, and to do and say clever things.

As a result, he sought refuge in greater eccentricities, and that was the beginning. That was what started him off on the cans.

Fergal felt he needed somewhere to hide, a wall to retreat behind — some shelter. He didn't want a hobby to bring him into contact with other people, he wanted one to shield him from them. And that was when he became interested in cans.

Not rare cans, though, nor ancient cans from expeditions to the North or South Pole; not foreign cans from exotic places, or cans in unusual colors. Just simple, ordinary, everyday cans.

Without labels.

***

Where and how he had got the idea, Fergal did not know. It just popped up, like a mushroom on the lawn. It hadn't been there yesterday — but today, there it was.

He had been in the supermarket with his mother, feeling bored and impatient, when his gaze had fallen onto a small display bin containing dented packets, bashed cornflakes boxes and items whose expiration date had either already passed or was fast approaching.

BARGAIN BASKET, a sign read. ALL ITEMS REDUCED.

Fergal picked a few of them up. Some of the bargain items seemed to have nothing wrong with them at all, they were just unpopular products that had never caught on.

Fergal picked up a plastic bottle and read the label.

BANANA-AND-CHEESE-FLAVORED MILK SHAKE.

He dropped it back into the bin.

Banana and *cheese*? *Eeuch!* No wonder nobody had bought it. Or if they had bought it once, they wouldn't buy it twice.

But then he saw something interesting, a flash of silver in the bottom of the bin. It lay half hidden under the crumpled cornflakes boxes and the soon-to-be-stale bread rolls. It lay like a trout among reeds and stones, at the bottom of a stream. It was the kind of flash of silver a fisherman might see as a fish comes along, just under the surface of the water, before it shimmers and darts away.

The kind he might try to tempt out with a fly or a juicy maggot on a hook.

He reached in. His hand closed around it.

He pulled it up out of the display bin and looked at it closely. It was a can. A simple, ordinary can. What made *this* one interesting was the simple fact that it didn't have a label.

All that was on the can was a small circular sticker, which read REDUCED and gave the price.

It was cheap. Very cheap. Just a few pennies, really. A bargain, in fact. Which doubtlessly was why it was sitting in the bargain basket.

"Mum . . ."

Mrs. Bamfield was just getting served at the delicatessen counter.

"What is it, Fergal?"

"What's this?"

"That can?"

"There's no label."

"I know. That's why it was in the bargain basket."

"Why?"

"The label must have come off somehow. You know, got torn off when it was being transported. Or it was never stuck on properly in the first place. So the supermarket sells them off cheaply."

"But what's in it?"

"That's just the point, Fergal. You don't know. That's why it's so cheap. You have to take a gamble."

A gamble. It crossed Fergal's mind that he had never actually taken a gamble before. He was too young to take gambles — the ordinary gambles that is: to buy scratch cards or lottery tickets, to go into betting shops or play the online casinos. But here was a real live gamble, just waiting to be taken.

His mother got what she wanted from the delicatessen counter — some pungent, suspiciously blue-looking cheese. She put her purchase into the trolley and moved on along the aisle. Fergal replaced the unlabeled can in the bargain basket and followed her. But his mind stayed with the can.

"Mum . . ."

"Yes?"

"What do you think could be in it?"

"What?"

"The can?"

"Can?"

"The one without the label, in the bargain basket?"

"Anything. Anything that you normally get in a can. Beans, olives, sweet corn, carrots, potatoes, peas, soup . . ."

"Tomato soup?" He liked tomato soup. "Do you think so?"

"Yes, it could be," she said. "It could be tomato soup. But then again, it might be dog food."

"Dog food?"

"Could be."

He wasn't so keen on the idea of dog food. But then a dog would be quite keen on the idea of dog food, so it wouldn't be wasted. Not that Fergal had a dog; he had a cat. But other people had dogs. He could give it to somebody else's dog. If he bought it, that was.

If.

Fergal kept thinking about the can, all the way around the supermarket. It was like a lucky dip, like taking a chance on the flip of a coin or the turn of a card, it was almost like living dangerously. It was practically an adventure.

In fact, it was an adventure — an adventure in a can. Because it could so easily go one way, or just as easily go another. You might find something delicious and surprising inside. Something wonderful, something you had never seen or tasted before.

Or it might be a bitter disappointment. It might be sweet corn, or boring old mushy peas.

Or it might be a can of sausages for hot dogs. Or a can of creamy rice pudding. Fergal knew that a lot of people didn't go in for rice pudding, but he personally loved the stuff. He wouldn't have minded a can of rice pudding, not at all.

But then again, it might be spinach.

Was there anything worse than canned spinach?

Except, perhaps, for two tins of canned spinach?

Eeeuch!

It might have been all right for Popeye the Sailor Man, and he was welcome to it. But imagine getting your silver bargain-basket can home and opening it up, your heart full of hope, your mind full of anticipation, only to peel the lid back to discover that it contained a mess of green soggy vegetables.

You'd be depressed for the rest of the week.

And yet . . . and yet. That moment of excitement. That moment of not knowing. That moment of hope before the moment of discovery. Had you or hadn't you won the lottery, that lottery of the cans?

It was too good to resist.

"Hang on, Mum, won't be a second."

They were nearly at the checkout, just about to join the line.

"Fergal! Where are you going? Fergal . . . don't disappear."

Ignoring her, he ran back down the aisle and arrived at the bargain basket, only to find an elderly lady there, slowly poring over all the cut-price items on offer.

Fergal watched her.

Please don't take the can, he willed her. *Please don't take the can.*

She reached out and took the can.

No, no! Don't buy it. Don't put it in your basket! Don't take the can!

She peered at it through her spectacles. Her mouth pursed into a hundred wrinkles. Did she or didn't she want the can? The matter seemed to require some thought.

It's mine, it's mine, it's mine, Fergal's brain silently yelled at her. *I saw it first and it's mine. Please don't put it into your shopping basket. Please don't take the can.*

She held the can next to her ear and she shook it. Fergal watched her. Yes, yes. He should have thought of that — shake and listen; listen and shake. Maybe this old lady was a bargain expert, maybe she knew what was worth having and this can was —

She put it back. She picked up a battered can of peaches with a dent in the side and put that into her shopping basket instead.

"Fergal!"

His mother was calling from the checkout. She was at the front of the line now, and their groceries were already moving along on the conveyor belt. Fergal grabbed the can and hurried to join her.

"What's that?"

"A can."

"But that's the one that doesn't have a label."

"I know."

"I don't want to buy that."

"I do, though. I'll pay for it out of my pocket money."

"What?" She looked at him, half surprised, half amused. "What are you going to do with it?"

"Keep it. Or open it. It all depends."

11

If Fergal hadn't had a reputation for being clever, his mother may well have insisted that he take the can back to where he had got it from. But as it was, she just regarded this latest display of eccentricity as one more facet of genius. She could almost hear herself telling the other mothers.

"Fergal's started collecting cans, you know."

"A collection can? Like for charity?"

"Oh no. Not a *collection* can. Not one for putting money in. He collects *cans*. With no labels on them."

"It must be because he's so clever."

"It must."

"You must be so proud of him — Fergal and his cans. And rightly so."

"Absolutely."

So she nodded indulgently and let the unlabeled can join all the other groceries on the conveyor belt. The checkout assistant held the silver can up to the scanner. There was a special bar code on the little REDUCED sticker, and the scanner bleeped as she passed the can through.

Fergal made a note of the cost. He took out his pocket money.

"Mum . . ."

"No, it's all right. I'll buy it for you."

But Fergal insisted that he be allowed to pay for it himself. It was going to be the start of his collection. That way it would truly be his and he wouldn't be indebted to anyone.

They left the supermarket and loaded the groceries into the car. Fergal took his can from one of the bags and sat in the passenger seat, with his seat belt around him, holding his can. He carefully removed the REDUCED sticker from it, rolled the sticker into a ball, and dropped it into the little rubbish holder in the car, next to the gear stick. He breathed on the silver surface of the can and polished it with his sleeve until it gleamed. His mother glanced at him and smiled tolerantly. Fergal. Him and his fads. Cans now. What would it be next? You never knew with Fergal.

"Are you going to open it when we get home," she asked, "and see what's inside?"

"Dunno," Fergal mumbled. And that was perfectly true, he didn't. He didn't know now whether he wanted to open it or not. Maybe there was an adventure inside, or maybe there wasn't. In some ways, he preferred the suspense and the mystery: better the thrill of uncertainty than the possible disappointment of knowing.

Maybe it was best to remain in the dark.

2. ONE CAN LEADS TO ANOTHER

Fergal had more or less agreed with himself that he wasn't going to open it. At least not immediately, not for a while, not until he had amassed a few more unlabeled cans for his collection. For one can on its own wasn't anywhere near a collection, neither were two, nor three, come to that, nor even four.

How many was a collection then? he wondered. A dozen or more? A minimum of twenty? Thirty? Forty? Forty-five?

Fergal was in his room; the can sat on his desk, shiny and silver and full of secrets. Sometimes he picked it up and weighed it in his hand. It felt heavy. So what did that mean? Did that give any indication as to the nature of its contents? No. Not really. Sometimes he held it to his ear and shook it, listening out for the sound of liquid moving about inside. That would mean it was soup. Or maybe not. Maybe it would mean it was canned mandarin oranges. But there was no slushing sound at all.

What could it be, then? Something nice? Something nasty? It only needed a can opener to find out.

And yet . . . why open it straightaway? Why open it at all? Why open it and risk disappointment? Wasn't it better in some ways not to open it? To go on speculating and dreaming and imagining what it might be? All sorts of things came in cans, after all. Even chocolate. Fergal had seen it, one Christmastime, there on the supermarket shelf — CANNED CHOCOLATE WORMS, a festive novelty.

Umm. Canned chocolate worms wouldn't be bad. They weren't real worms, after all. Not real worms dipped in chocolate. That would be disgusting.

Fergal held the can to his nose. It smelled like a can. Nothing of its contents leaked out, no telltale whiff of what lay under the metal. The can kept its secrets, its vacuum-packed secrets, and it would go on keeping them until somebody wielded a can opener and uncovered them all.

Fergal held the can to the light. He looked at himself in the metal. His distorted features looked back at him. He seemed like a figure in a tiny hall of mirrors, small and absurd.

He could hear the voices already. "*That Fergal, he's a deep one. Collects cans without any labels on them, you know.*"

Yes, that was all he would have to do — just go on collecting. Instantly the pressure was off him. He wouldn't have to say anything clever or do anything clever again to live up to other people's expectations. He could relax and be himself. He could hide behind his cans.

"*Hi, Fergal, how are the cans?*"

"*Find anything interesting in the cans today, Fergal?*"

"*He's a clever one, that Fergal, you know, spends all his pocket money on cans.*"

When his mother was out in the garden, he took the can downstairs and weighed it on the kitchen scales. He made a note of the weight and wrote it down in a spare notebook. He first ruled out several columns, and in the initial column he wrote the date (March 23) and in the second column the weight of the can (8 ounces). To the left of these figures he wrote "Can Number One." He then went to a kitchen drawer and took out a sheet of small stickers that his mother used for labeling the things she cooked and put into the freezer. He peeled off a small circular sticker and wrote "No. 1" on it. He then attached this to the base of the can and went back up to his room.

He wondered if there was a magazine for can collectors. *Can Collectors' Weekly* or *Tin Can Gazette*. You could get magazines for practically everything else. All kinds of collectors had their magazines — stamp collectors, coin collectors, model-railway enthusiasts, you name it.

He went out to the newsstand to see what was there.

Nothing.

"Excuse me, would you have any magazines for people who collect cans?"

The shopkeeper gave him a blank look, as if Fergal was either exceptionally intelligent or nuts. As popular opinion tended toward the former, he was inclined to go along with it.

"Sorry, son," he said. "There's no such magazine — not that I know of. I've never heard of anyone collecting cans before. Sorry. You could always look on the Internet."

So Fergal took his advice and looked on the Internet, but there were no Web sites for can collectors either. He seemed to be in a class of his own.

***

Fergal still didn't open the can.

"Not opening it, Fergal?" his mother asked him, perhaps a little curious herself about what was inside.

"No."

"Not going to open it at all?"

"Might do. Later. Not today, though."

That evening Fergal showed the can to his father. Mr. Bamfield did his best to pretend to admire it, but you could tell that he wasn't really impressed.

"Very nice, Fergal, a very nice . . . can."

"It's good, isn't it, Dad?"

"Yes, very nice. Only . . ."

"Only?"

"Only what does it *do*, exactly?"

"Well, it doesn't do anything, Dad. It just is."

"Just *is*?"

"Yes."

"Right. Well, that's very nice. I'll leave you to it, then."

When his father had gone, Fergal felt decidedly irritated with him. After all, you didn't say to somebody who collected stamps, "What does that stamp *do*, exactly?" It didn't have to *do* anything to be worth collecting. It just had to *be*. So why wasn't that good enough for cans?

But that was grown-ups for you — always being picky.

Fergal put the can on the top shelf of his bookcase and it remained there for the rest of the week. The following weekend, when his mother set off to do the weekly supermarket shopping, Fergal insisted on accompanying her. So they drove off once again to the same supermarket as before, the one they always went to, and as soon as they had got themselves a trolley and walked inside, Fergal made a beeline for the bargain basket.

He was disappointed. There was nothing there. Or rather there was plenty there, plenty of bargains that is, plenty of battered boxes, plenty of dented cans with torn labels still on, but of cans with *no* labels, there was not a solitary one.

Fergal rummaged through the bargain basket several times, just in case there was an unlabeled can in there and he had missed it. But there wasn't and he hadn't. He hung around it for a while, eyeing the passing shop assistants and shelf stockers as they came into the supermarket through the flapping doors leading to the adjoining storage warehouse, hoping that they might bring some silver cans with them and drop them into the bargain bin. But no. Nothing. Just a packet of noodles near its sell-by date, reduced to half price.

He went to find his mother. Their trolley was already half full.

"Where have you been, Fergal?"

"Oh, nowhere. Just looking around."

They walked on past the boxes of cereal and put a few more items into the trolley.

"What's the matter, Fergal? You're very quiet this morning."

"Oh, nothing.

"Mum . . ."

"Yes, Fergal?"

"Do you think it's time we started shopping in another supermarket?"

"Another supermarket? Whatever for? We've been coming to this one for years."

"It just doesn't seem as good as it used to be."

"Oh, really? In what way?"

"It just doesn't seem to have as good a selection as it used to."

"As good a selection of what?"

"Oh, you know . . . cans."

"Cans?"

"Yes, cans."

Fergal's mother gave him one of her looks. She wondered sometimes if Fergal wasn't just a bit *too* clever. A bit too clever for his own good. For everybody's good, come to that.

"Well, I'm sorry, Fergal," she said, "but I've always found this supermarket extremely good. And what's more, I've got lots of points on my customer loyalty card, which entitles me to all sorts of bargains, so we're going to stick with this one."

And that was that, as far as Fergal's mother was concerned. But in Fergal's opinion, that was not that at all.

If anything, it was a turning point, the moment when he decided he would have to take can hunting into his own hands.

***

Fergal's family lived within walking distance of his school, and — weather and time permitting — he was occasionally allowed to make his own way there and back. He began to take advantage of these opportunities to pop into the local shops he passed to search their bargain baskets for cans. Some shops didn't even seem to have bargain baskets. Others did, but they had no unlabeled cans in them, and Fergal would go away disappointed again.

Then they started appearing. It seemed a case of famine or feast. For weeks on end there would be no cans at all, then three or four would show up together. Sometimes even six or seven, more than he could afford to buy. Gradually Fergal's collection of cans began to grow larger.

Soon, to his mother's increasing unease, Fergal had filled the entire top shelf of his bookcase with cans. There they stood, polished, unlabeled, each with a little sticker with its number on it, each with its details written in the notebook (marked CANS), giving weight, date of purchase, and dimensions.

Fergal varied the arrangement of the cans to suit his mood. Sometimes he arranged them from largest to smallest, then he rearranged them smallest to largest, then he might arrange them by number, starting with the one he had first purchased and leading up to the most recent acquisition.

When his collection reached twenty-five cans, his parents decided that it was time to speak to him.

"Don't you think, Fergal," his mother said, as tactfully as possible, "that you maybe have enough cans now? Or, perhaps, before you go buying some more, it might be a good idea to open one or two of the ones you have already, just to see what's inside of them, and maybe to make a bit of room?"

Only Fergal didn't really want to. The longer he had the cans, the harder it became to open any of them. In some ways the unopened cans were like money. To open them would be to spend them, and then he wouldn't have the money anymore. Anyway, if he were to open one, which one would it be?

So Fergal went on looking and he went on finding and he went on buying and he went on bringing home, until finally his collection of cans without labels filled up three of the shelves on his bookcase, and his books were all stacked on the windowsill.

In total he now had forty-eight cans, and it had taken only a few months to collect them all. Then, one Friday, he brought home yet another can, and his mother decided to put her foot down.

"No more cans, Fergal. I'm sorry, but I absolutely must insist. I can't have your bedroom turning into a supermarket, getting more and more cluttered up with cans. You'll be bringing home a trolley and a couple of wire baskets next."

"It's not cluttered, Mum. My cans are all neatly stacked up in the bookcase."

"Yes, and it is intended to *be* a bookcase, Fergal. It's not a *can-case*, it's a *bookcase* and, as its name implies, you are supposed to keep *books* in it. Not a load of old cans. So no more of them."

"Just one, Mum."

"No."

"Just one, and then I'll have an even number. I've only got an odd number at the moment."

She thought about it, then gave in.

"All right. You can have one more can, Fergal. But only one. If you want any more cans after that, you have to get rid of an old one first before you can get a new one. Is that a deal?"

"Okay," Fergal said reluctantly. "Deal."

It wasn't really the deal he wanted. But he could see it was the best he was going to get.

***

One more can. Just one more can. If Fergal could buy only one more can, then he would have to be selective about it. When you could only have one more can, then you didn't want just any old can. You wanted one that was a bit different, a bit unusual in some way. A can among cans, that was what you wanted. A can of distinction. A can with personality.

So, like a true collector, Fergal became very choosy. It wasn't enough now for a can simply to have no label and to be in the bargain basket. It had to have extra qualities, fresh dimensions.

Weeks went by. Fergal came across several unlabeled cans in that time, but they all looked remarkably similar to the forty-nine cans he already had. His collection was fairly diverse in that some cans were small, some were large, some were heavy, and some were light. Most were shiny, some were dull, some were tall, some had a ring-pull on the top, others could only be opened with a can opener. But to find a different kind of can was like looking for a rare stamp.

And then he found it. The moment he picked it up, he knew he was on to something. Something strange and unique and extraordinary.

It wasn't an unusual shape; in fact, it was quite a standard size. He hadn't even been going to bother with it, it looked so ordinary. He had only gone to move it out of the way to see if there were any other cans hidden underneath it in the bargain basket. Only when he picked it up, he immediately realized that here was a can with a difference.

For one thing, it was lighter than all the others he had come across. Far, far lighter. This was definitely no ordinary can of beans or soup or stewed steak or curried chicken or macaroni and cheese. This was a can which felt so light that it could almost have been empty. But despite being so light, it definitely had something inside it. Fergal knew that much for certain.

Because when he shook the can, it rattled.

3. CAN IN, CAN OUT

Some cans made hardly any sound at all when you shook them. Their contents remained immobile, for there was no room inside for them to wobble about. Other cans had one of two basic noises: a solid, heavy tone, and a liquid, slurpy one.

But a rattle, that was odd.

Fergal felt his skin prickle with the thrill of success. But there was another sensation too — a tingle of apprehension, a mild shudder of fear and foreboding.

He picked the can up and looked around. Was anyone else coming? Was anybody heading for the bargain basket, anxious to get to the cans? No. Nobody. It was his. All he had to do was to pay for it.

Clutching the can tightly, he hurried to the checkout and placed the can down on the conveyor. The lady at the till picked the can up as it approached her.

"This for you?"

Fergal nodded.

"It's light, isn't it?"

He nodded again, worried that she would take the can from him, or refuse to sell it to him on the grounds that its contents might be dangerous, or unsuitable for a boy of his age.

"It rattles," the till lady said.

"Mmmm . . ." Fergal vaguely agreed.

He watched with apprehension as she held the can to her ear and shook it.

"Not too hard," he wanted to say. "Not too hard. You might break it."

The lady looked at the can for the price sticker.

"No bar code on this one," she said.

She consulted a list of price codes next to her till and put the can without the label through under the heading *Miscellaneous*. Fergal paid her for it with his pocket money.

"Carrier bag, dear?"

"No, thank you."

"There's your change, then. Enjoy your can."

Fergal left the shop and hurried home, clutching the can tightly. Every now and again he gave it a small shake, just to hear and to feel the rattle of whatever was inside.

What could it be? And why was it so light? Had something maybe gone wrong in the canning process, back at the factory, on the production line?

The can should have been filled up, but only a squirt had come out of the filling nozzle. Due to a blockage, perhaps. Then the can had moved on along the conveyor belt and had somehow been missed by quality control.

Next the label had got torn or had peeled off in transit or in handling, so eventually the can had ended up in the bargain basket. And now Fergal had it. Only what was inside?

Then Fergal thought of another theory — the can was *supposed* to be like that. It was *supposed* to rattle. It hadn't ended up that way by mistake at all. It was a novelty of some kind. He'd seen canned underwear for sale sometimes, canned boxers, canned briefs, canned socks, the kind of daft presents you gave to people for Christmas or on their birthdays.

Once he had even seen a can purporting to contain Scotch Mist, and the label had said that the can contained "Genuine, Early Morning Mist, Collected from the Glens of Scotland and Canned While Still Fresh."

Some people would buy anything.

***

"Got another can there, Fergal?"

Fergal's father was out cleaning the car. He glanced at Fergal's new can with doubt and disapproval.

"Erm, yes, Dad."

"This is going to be the last one, isn't it?"

"Erm . . . yes, Dad. I suppose so."

"Unless you get rid of another one first, all right? If you want to buy any more, you have to get rid of one beforehand. No more than fifty in total. Fifty cans with no labels are more than enough cans for anyone."

"Yes, Dad."

Fergal didn't know if he really agreed though. Some people stored up hundreds of cans. They hoarded them so that they'd be all right if a disaster ever happened — if famine came or a war broke out. Fergal had wondered how long he and his family would last if there weren't any supermarkets. About a week, he reckoned, then all their food would be gone, and they'd be out digging up mushrooms.

You'll be glad I've got my cans if a hurricane ever comes or there's an invasion by aliens, Fergal thought as he left his father washing the car.

He went to his room and set the new can down on his desk. He polished it with his sleeve, determined its circumference with his mother's borrowed tape measure and entered its details into his Cans Book. Then he took it down to the kitchen and weighed it on the electronic scales.

It was the lightest yet, the lightest of all the fifty cans. A record, in fact. A record-breaking can.

Fergal felt a momentary pang of longing. He wished he had someone to share his hobby with, a fellow collector, who would experience the same rush of adrenaline, the same flow of excitement and curiosity, the same sense of mystery and exploration.

Finding a can like this, it was almost like discovering America or venturing out into space, like being one of the great explorers — boldly going where no one had gone before.

"Hello, Fergal."

His mother came in to fill up a small watering can from the cold tap. It was time for her to water her houseplants.

"How are you?"

"Fine thanks, Mum."

"And what have you been doing?"

"Shopping, Mum." He hesitatingly held out the silver object for her to see. "I've got a new can."

She barely glanced at it.

"Yes, very nice, dear."

Then she turned off the tap and left, heading for the sitting room and her house plant.

"*Yes, very nice, dear!*"

Fergal watched her go with resentment smoldering inside him.

"*We're talking cans here, Mum!*" he wanted to shout after her. "*We're talking important cans. We're talking rare and unusual rattling-type cans. We're talking deep and meaningful cans of mysterious contents, the kinds of cans which, once opened, could maybe even change your whole life. And all you have to do is to fetch the opener and clamp it on the edge of the can, then turn the butterfly handle until the lid is all but cut off, save for one little bit. Then you look down into the very can itself, and its contents are revealed. And what you see is . . .*"

What?

What did you see? What would you see? Only if Fergal did open the can, it wouldn't be a secret surprise anymore. It might be nothing but a great big disappointment. So which was it better to have? The mystery and the speculation, or the certain knowledge and the possible dismay?

Fergal couldn't decide. He made a note of the weight of the can in his Cans Book, then he took it back up to his room and added it to his shelf.

He lay back on his bed and admired his collection — fifty cans, all without labels; some were silver, some dull gray, some with ridges, some without. Fifty little mysteries, fifty conundrums, fifty puzzles waiting to be solved.

"No more cans, Fergal. That's the last. If you want any more, you'll have to open one and get rid of it and let the new one replace it. No more. Fifty is quite enough."

It would be a shame to give up his collecting now though. No more prowling through the supermarkets like some private detective on an important case. . . .

All right, then. He'd get rid of one so that he could have the pleasure of buying another. Which one would it be?

He closed his eyes tight.

Eeeny, meeny, miney, mo . . .

He opened one eye and looked at where his finger pointed.

That one? That can? The big, round one that looked as if it might contain a sponge pudding?

No. Maybe not. Maybe not after all. Go again.

Eeeny, meeny, miney . . .

That one then? The other one? The squat, fat, looks-like-somebody-sat-on-it one?

No, perhaps not. On second thought, maybe not that one either. Go again.

Eeeny, meeny, miney, mo,
Catch a tiger by his toe,
If he hollers let him go,
Eeeny, meeny, miney . . .
Mo!

His finger stopped moving. He opened his eyes. The *eeeny-meeny* had chosen the new one. The most interesting one of all. That was it, he had decided. He would stay with the one that fate had chosen for him. He would open the new one.

He picked the can back up from the shelf, he held it carefully, and he made his way down to the kitchen.

The coast was clear. His father had finished washing the car and was starting to polish it. His mother had gone out to plant some shrubs at the far end of the garden. Angus the cat was outside, perched on the kitchen windowsill, peering in at him with curiosity. Fergal rapped on the glass and the cat ran off.

Fergal opened a drawer and took out the butterfly can opener. He hadn't used can openers very much, although he had seen it done often enough. He couldn't get the cutter to pierce the metal on his first two attempts, but then he got the hang of it, and slowly the can began to open as he twisted the wings of the steel butterfly around. Metal parted from metal, a dark gash opened in the top. Round the opener went, all but completing the circle. As he knew from the weight that there was only something small inside, he didn't bother to lever the lid up, he just pressed it down inside. He upturned the can, and let its contents drop to the kitchen counter.

Then he looked. And he saw. He felt both excitement and wonder and the slight metallic taste of fear. Lying there, on the top of the kitchen counter, was the last thing in the world he had ever expected to see, the last thing he had ever expected to fall out of the can.

It was gold.

4. FINDERS KEEPERS

Fergal suddenly felt guilty. He glanced out of the window again, to make sure that neither his mother nor father was on the way back into the house. Rightly or wrongly, he sensed that this was something he had to keep to himself. Why exactly, he did not know. But in some curious way it was almost as if he had done something wrong; as if instead of finding the gold he had stolen it.

But, finders keepers, losers weepers. Wasn't that right?

He reached out and touched it with his finger. It was a piece of jewelry of some kind. It was small, quite plain, and with a sharp point to it on one side, as if it was designed to pin through or to fasten into something. Fergal picked the small object up and dropped it into the palm of his left hand. He examined it closely and moved it around, seeing it from all angles. He wondered how valuable it was. Maybe not all that much on its own, it was too small. But if he had ten of them, twenty, fifty, a hundred — well, they'd be worth something then.

He saw that the empty can was still sitting on the kitchen surface. He dropped it into the recycling box, then took the small gold object out into the garden. He had decided it would be safe to show it to other people after all, just as long as he didn't say where it had come from.

"Mum . . ."

He found her kneeling down by the flower beds. She looked up and smiled.

"Hello, Fergal."

"Mum, what's this?"

He opened his hand and held it out for her to see.

"What's that you've got?"

"I don't know."

"Let me see. Umm. Where did you get it from?"

"Oh, just found it," Fergal quite truthfully said.

"Well, it's not mine. I can tell you that. Because I don't have pierced ears. And it's certainly not your dad's."

"Pierced ears?"

"Yes. It's a sleeper."

"What's that?"

"Oh, you know, a kind of small earring. When people first have their ears pierced, they wear them to stop the hole from closing up. They're not uncomfortable to have in, not the way large earrings might be when you put your head on the pillow. So you can keep them in overnight. Which is why they call them sleepers."

"I see."

Fergal looked at the small gold stud.

"So it's a lady's then, is it?"

His mother smiled.

"Not necessarily," she said. "Lots of men have pierced ears too. And it might not be from an ear. Some people have their noses pierced, or their lips, their tongues even . . . and a whole lot of other things that I won't even mention."

The stud seemed to squirm on Fergal's hand. It was the mention of pierced noses and punctured lips that had done it. Somebody else's ears weren't too bad, but other people's lips and noses were a bit too personal. Belly buttons fleetingly crossed his mind.

"Is it valuable?" he asked.

"Well . . ." His mother reached out and picked the stud up. "Not very, I wouldn't imagine. It is gold, but such a small amount . . ."

"But if you had ten of them?"

"Where are you going to get ten of them from?"

"Or a hundred?"

"A hundred!"

"I mean, they'd be worth something then? If you melted them all down, say?"

"Yes, I suppose they would. Why?"

"Oh . . . just wondering."

Fergal put his hand out to receive the stud back, but his mother held on to it. It seemed to look more gold than ever in contrast to the maroon rubber of her gardening gloves.

"So where did you find it?"

"Oh . . ."

He still didn't like to say. Not about the can, somehow. There were things adults would accept, and things they wouldn't, no matter how true they were.

But it wasn't just the fear of not being believed that held Fergal back. It was more that he simply didn't want his mother, or anyone else, to know. It was his. His mystery. His secret. His adventure. And he didn't want anyone — and especially not an adult — interfering.

He played for time to think. "Sorry, Mum? What did you say?"

"I said, where did you find it?"

"Find it?"

"Yes."

"The gold stud?"

"Yes."

He didn't want to tell her, but at the same time, he didn't want to lie. There is truth that reveals and truth that conceals, and right now he needed the second kind.

"I, er, found it in the supermarket."

"Oh."

"On the shelf."

"Oh," his mother said. She held the stud up between her finger and thumb and raised it to the light.

"Do you think I should take it back?" Fergal asked. "Or hand it in? To the supermarket lost property? Or maybe even take it down to the police station?"

His mother laughed and dropped the gold stud back into his outstretched hand.

"No, I don't think so, Fergal. It's such a small thing. I shouldn't think anyone would go back for that, or even know where they had lost it. No. They'd just assume it was gone for good and go buy another one."

"I can keep it then?" Fergal said, a slight tremor of excitement in his voice.

"I don't see why not."

"Thanks, Mum."

"Don't thank me. You found it."

He turned to go back into the house, but his mother called to him.

"Oh, Fergal . . ."

He froze. What was she going to say? To tell him to return it to the supermarket after all?

"Yes, Mum?"

"Be careful with it. Mind the sharp point. We don't want it sticking into your finger or anything."

"Don't worry, Mum. I'll be careful."

He went on into the kitchen and closed the door behind him. He took the stud to the sink and rinsed it under the hot tap.

Even if it had come out of someone's nose, now it was clean.

Then he took the stud up to his room and placed it on a piece of writing paper on his desk.

He peered at the gold sleeper through his magnifying glass, in the vague hope that there might be initials on it, in tiny, microscopic writing, engraved into the soft metal. But there was nothing. Nothing whatever to indicate the identity of its owner. Not one single, solitary clue.

Questions, questions, questions. There had to be an answer to them. For every problem, a solution; for every mystery, an explanation.

Explanation

He wrote the word at the top of the paper and then he underlined it. There had to be one. The gold stud hadn't climbed inside the can all on its own.

He put down a subheading.

Questions.

That was the way to do it. Questions came before explanations sure as lightning came before thunder.

Question: How did the stud get into the can?

Answer: It fell out of somebody's ear.

Question: Whose ear?

Answer: Someone who worked in the factory.

Question: What factory?

Answer: The factory that makes the cans of whatever stuff it is that should have been in there.

Question: What factory is that?

Answer: Don't know and don't have any way of finding out that I can see.

Question: Why was the can empty apart from the stud? Surely the stud should have been mixed up with the contents? Beans or peas or olives or whatever it might be.

Answer: Don't know.

Fergal put his pen down and looked thoughtfully at the gold stud again. He had gone as far as he could go and he hadn't really got anywhere. He wished he had someone to talk to about it. Two heads were better than one, and they might have solved the mystery between them, but one head was all he had. If he had a friend, somebody who shared his interest and his hobby, it would be different. But there was nobody, just him. It was a shame that no one else was even remotely interested in the mysteries of cans.

He looked across the room to his computer. There was always the Internet, of course . . .

Fergal booted the machine up and went online. He put a bulletin up in the chat room he used occasionally.

Nerdy-Boy: Anyone here interested in cans?

(Nerdy-Boy was his user name. He had decided it was best to say it before anyone else did.)

He didn't have to wait long for an answer.

Talk-To-The-Hand: Hey, Nerdy-Boy? What do you mean about cans? I go to the can sometimes. That any good?
Nerdy-Boy: That isn't what I mean.
CinnyBuff8: Hey, Nerdy, if you don't mean the can, do you mean the cancan? I'm learning that at dancing class.
Nerdy-Boy: No. Not the cancan! Just cans!
CinnyBuff8: Cans of what?
Nerdy-Boy: Just cans of anything. And empty cans.
Talk-To-The-Hand: Hey, Nerdy-Boy, shouldn't you be Crazy-Boy? Why do you buy empty cans? Are you slimming?
Nerdy-Boy: I mean almost empty cans. Cans that have things in them that aren't on the label.
Missie-Daisey: So what is on the label?
Nerdy-Boy: There is no label. That's what I mean.

Talk-To-The-Hand: Nerdy-Boy, you need help. Suggest you get some therapy. Maybe you might get some in a can. Can you? Geddit?

Nerdy-Boy: Ha ha. Very funny. I don't think.

The chat-room conversation moved on after that to ring tones and new Web sites and check-out-this-band suggestions. But Fergal wasn't interested, so he signed off. He had other things on his mind. Shiny metal things.

Because now that he had opened and emptied one can . . .

. . . it was time to get another.

But first he needed to put the gold stud somewhere safe. He opened a drawer and buried it under his winter sweaters. Nobody would disturb it there for a while, not even his mother. Surely he'd have found an explanation for it long before winter came.

"Another one? I thought we had an agreement, Fergal."

It was Saturday, and it was supermarket time again. "I know we did."

"No more cans. You weren't to buy another can until you'd first opened and got rid of one."

"Well, I did."

"Did you?"

"Yes."

His mother looked at him dubiously as she loaded a bottle of washing-machine liquid into the trolley.

"You can count them if you like when we get home."

"I believe you. So when did you open it?"

"Oh, the other day."

"I didn't know you'd opened one. You never mentioned it."

"Didn't I?"

"I don't think so. So what was in it?"

"What?"

"The can you opened. What was in it?"

"Oh . . . nothing much."

He still didn't want to tell her. He didn't know why. He just didn't.

"There must have been something in it. What was it? SpaghettiOs? Peaches? Pineapple chunks?"

"Oh, something like that."

"Did you eat it?"

"Er . . . no."

"That was a bit of a waste."

"Sorry."

"Well, don't throw it away next time. Dad or I might like whatever's in there."

"Okay. So can I get another one?"

"Oh, very well. If you must."

"Good."

"But it's a weird hobby, Fergal. Very weird. You wouldn't like to start collecting something else instead, I suppose?"

"No. I'm happy with cans."

"Well, I dare say it comes from being clever."

"Yes, Mum. I guess it does."

She went off to fill up the supermarket trolley while Fergal headed for the bargain bin.

There were three cans without labels in the bargain basket that day, but they all felt heavy and solid. Two of them squished when shaken, the other gave a faint but solid thud, as though a big slab of meat was inside. Maybe it was a chunk of Spam, moving around in a cushion of jelly.

Eeuch!

He rejoined his mother at the checkout.

"Didn't you get anything?" she asked.

"Decided against it. I didn't see anything that appealed to me. Nothing I haven't got already."

"Oh."

Mrs. Bamfield didn't comment further, but she felt relieved. Maybe the cans craze was finally over.

Five weeks went by. Five weeks of combing through the bargain baskets of every shop he passed. It didn't matter whether it was a huge supermarket or a small corner store.

Sometimes Fergal grew discouraged and almost gave up. The constant looking and the endless disappointment wore him down. Maybe it wasn't such a good hobby after all, especially when you had nobody to share it with. If there had been a society of can collectors, who held meetings where they told each other stories about "Cans I have known" and "Interesting things I have found in cans" and "Can-finding holidays I have been on, both at home and abroad," and who held Can-swapping events and Rare-can Afternoons, then it would have been different. But as the weeks went by, Fergal grew increasingly discouraged, as nothing of interest emerged from the bargain baskets he so assiduously rummaged through.

"I'll give it one more week," he eventually decided, "and I'm going to pack it in. I'm going to get rid of my whole collection. I'm going to open up the lot, all forty-nine cans, and find out what's inside each one. Then I'll eat the good stuff, give what I don't like to anyone who fancies it, and feed the rest to the cat. Then I'll take up a more normal hobby, like collecting fossils or foreign coins."

So Saturday came. It was make-or-break time. And something happened to make Fergal change his mind.

He found something. A can with a difference. It was there in the bargain basket, a perfectly ordinary-seeming can, still sticky where the label had once been.

He picked it up. It was light. Too light. Far, far too light. Far lighter than a can was supposed to be. He shook it. Maybe it was another gold stud? Maybe it was the other one, the other half of the pair? Maybe somehow both studs had ended up in cans.

No. It wasn't that kind of noise. It wasn't the rattle of a hard, metallic object. It was a softer, much duller sound, something like . . . what?

He held the can to his ear and shook it again gently, not too viciously, in case he damaged what was inside.

"Help you, sir?"

For an astonishing moment he thought the can had spoken to him, but he looked up to see that the voice belonged to one of the supermarket staff, who had plainly been watching Fergal for a while and must have thought that he was acting suspiciously. The man was dressed in the uniform of a security guard.

"Help you at all, sir?"

Fergal knew enough to know that when adults started calling you "sir," it was time to be on your way.

"No, no. I'm all right, thank you."

"Wishing to buy that, are you, sir?" the man asked him.

Fergal saw that he was still holding the can. The man must have thought that he meant to steal it.

"Y-yes, I am," he stuttered.

"Then you'll be wanting to take it to the till and pay for it then, won't you, sir?"

"Y-yes, that's right, I will."

Fergal realized then that he hadn't picked up a wire basket. That was probably why he looked so suspicious — going around without a basket or a trolley, he must have looked like a young shoplifter.

"I'll go and pay for it now."

He hurried toward the checkout, feeling in his coat for his pocket money as he went. He joined the line and paid for the can.

"Is that all, dear?"

"Yes, thank you."

She rang up the price of the can without the label.

"Got a bargain there."

"I hope so."

"There's your change."

"Thanks."

He stood on the other side of the line of checkouts, holding his can and clutching carefully on to the receipt, so that people would know that the can had been paid for.

His mother appeared, pushing a trolley stacked near to overflowing.

"Fergal, what are you doing over there?" she called.

"Found a can," he called back. "Thought I'd better pay for it."

"Well, come over here and help me with these groceries."

Reluctantly, Fergal went back to help her, fearful of being accused of not having paid for his can. But his mother joined the line for the same cashier, and so she knew that he had.

"Likes his cans," she said to Mrs. Bamfield, nodding in Fergal's direction. The groceries ran off the conveyor belt and slid down the incline to be packed.

"He collects them," Fergal's mother explained.

"Oh, fancy," the cashier said. "He must be intelligent, then."

"Yes." Mrs. Bamfield nodded. "He is."

Well, you had to be, to collect cans.

Any fool knew that.

**

Fergal insisted on carrying his new can home personally, although his mother offered him space in one of her shopping bags.

"Put it in here if you like, Fergal."

"No thanks, Mum. I'm all right."

He held the can in his hands, resting it on his lap. As the car drove over bumps and the occasional pothole, he could feel its contents judder around inside.

Whatever could it be? Not another gold stud, definitely. But maybe something valuable just the same. Something softer, something with a dull, soft thud to it. Money, perhaps? A wad of money? A tight roll of folded notes, done up with a rubber band?

"Fergal?"

"Sorry, Mum? Did you say something?"

He'd even forgotten that she was in the car.

"Daydreaming again, Fergal."

"Must have been. Sorry. What was it?"

"I said, what would you like for lunch?"

"Sorry, didn't hear you."

"I could see that. So what do you want for lunch?"

"Not bothered."

"How about opening one of your cans?"

He turned and looked at her. What was she suggesting?

"Open one of my cans?"

"You could have one of them for lunch. Take pot luck. It might be something nice. If you wanted to, we could open the new one."

He felt a surge of panic. If anyone was to open the can, it was to be him, him alone, opening it alone. No one else was to see or to know anything.

"Oh, no. I don't want to open the new one, not straightaway."

"Okay. Well, maybe open one of the others, then?"

"Maybe, but not today. I think I'd just like grilled cheese."

His mother gave him a look, one of her is-this-latest-hobby-of-yours-such-a-good-idea? looks, but she didn't nag him about it.

"Okay. Grilled cheese it is, then. And what are you going to do this afternoon? Play on the computer?"

But the Internet seemed bland and uninteresting today, compared to . . . well . . . to, you know . . .

"No, I don't think I'll bother. Not today."

"Homework, then?"

"No. Do it tomorrow. I think I'll just . . . spend the afternoon . . . with my cans."

His mother's lips grew tighter, into a tense, compressed smile. "*Clever or not, Fergal,"* her face seemed to say, *"I'm getting worried about you and your cans. These cans have nearly gone too far."*

But they hadn't quite got there yet. Fergal's mother's patience may have been stretched, but it hadn't snapped. There was still a little elasticity left; it would stretch a little bit more.

***

After lunch Fergal went up to his room. Some minutes later, the front door banged shut, then a car started and he heard his father drive away. Then the back door opened and closed. He looked out down into the garden. His mother was crossing the lawn, carrying a little rubber mat for kneeling on, along with a trowel, some shears, and a tray of seedlings.

Good.

It was safe.

Fergal took his new can and went downstairs. In his other hand he carried his Cans Book.

He got out the kitchen scales and placed them on a level surface. He set the can down on them and noted its weight in his exercise book. It was much lighter than a regular can, but heavier than the one that had contained the gold stud. He didn't need to measure the dimensions of the can; he could tell from looking at it what size it was. There were really only a few standard sizes, and by now he could recognize them all at a glance.

Right.

He put the scales away and took out the can opener. He pressed the cutter next to the ridge of the can, then went to close it, to make it bite into the metal of the lid.

But something stopped him. Some feeling, some sixth sense. He looked out of the window. His mother had plainly forgotten something, or she wanted a glass of water to drink, but she was returning to the house.

He grabbed the can and the opener, left the kitchen, and hurried up to his room. He closed the door quietly and waited. Her voice called up the stairs.

"Fergal?"

Quietly now, casually, as if everything was fine.

"You okay?"

"I'm okay."

"What are you doing?"

"Playing with my cans."

"Oh, all right then. If the phone rings or if you want me, I'll be outside."

"Okay, Mum."

He went to the window. She was walking back out into the garden, carrying a small radio. He heard the faint sound of classical music. She never put the radio on loud in the garden. She didn't like to give the neighbors anything to complain about.

"Playing with my cans."

Why had he said that? It made it sound as though he had been stacking them up like building blocks. But maybe it had been the best thing to say. Adults didn't worry when you were just playing with something. It meant you didn't take it too seriously.

Right. Try again.

He set the can down on his desk. Even though it had no label, it was fairly easy to tell top from bottom. Bottoms and tops often had a different shape to them. All cans had markings too, codes and date stamps, and these were frequently — though not invariably — on the bottom of the can.

Fergal lifted the can and set a piece of paper under it, just in case the contents proved to be something messy. Best to be safe. Then he began again to open the can. He squeezed the cutters tightly into the ridge of the rim. They bit. There was a slight sigh as the vacuum inside the can was broken and the air rushed in. Then he turned the wheels with the wings of the butterfly, until the lid was cut all the way around apart from a tiny sliver of metal, which he had left uncut.

He shut his eyes. He gingerly felt for the can. He prized back the lid and twisted it off, being careful not to cut his fingers. He set the lid down somewhere on the desk. Then with his eyes still closed, he placed the can slowly onto its side, then quickly upturned it, before the contents could spill out. Then he opened his eyes again.

Now then. Moment of truth. Fergal reached forward, grasped the can and slowly lifted it up.

Something slid out onto the paper on the desk. Fergal had to study it for several seconds before he knew what it was. In truth, maybe he knew instantly, but it took time for his brain to believe his eyes. It was so improbable, so impossible, so not what he had expected.

Of all the things he had thought to find in the can, he had never imagined anything like this.

He stared at it, swallowing hard. Maybe he could put it back into the can and try again. Empty it out once more, and this time something else, something more reasonable, would appear.

But of course he couldn't.

If only he hadn't opened it. If only he had just kept the can in his collection. If only he had never discovered it in the bargain basket. If only he had never become interested in cans.

If only.

But it was far too late for if only.

It was a finger. A finger. A human finger. With a slightly grubby fingernail, and a mark around it — a faint indentation around the base.

There it was, lying on his desk.

One canned finger.

One finger, canned.

He sat there stunned, unable to move from his chair. He reached out to touch it, and then recoiled. He couldn't, not with his bare hands, not touch this dead, gruesome object.

Only then it occurred to him that it wasn't real. It was wax, or plastic. That was it. Something in a can for Halloween, maybe. Yes. That would be it. That would explain it. Okay, so it wasn't Halloween for a while, but maybe the can had been left over, it had rolled under a shelf somewhere, its label had come off, and it had ended up in the bargain basket.

That made sense. It was a gimmick, a trick. Halloween in a can.

There had probably been a whole range of them: Canned Eyeballs and Canned Toes and Canned Teeth.

Maybe it was *edible*. Perhaps it was made out of sugar. Or marzipan. A marzipan finger. There was only one way to find out — touch it, taste it, take a bite.

A bite? Take a bite? An actual bite? Of that finger?

Fergal wasn't so sure about that. He reached and took a pencil and gave the finger a prod. Well, at least it wasn't alive, that was one thing.

He peered at it cautiously, examining where it appeared to have been severed from the hand to which it had once belonged.

Hmm. They'd done a good job there, he thought. A very convincing piece of confectionery, right enough. The way they had got the pink sugar paste to simulate dried blood — very lifelike.

And the skillful manner in which the little veins stood out — most authentic.

And that grubby, half-chewed fingernail was a nice touch too.

And was that actually a little sugar wart there?

And look, the tip even had the whorls and spirals of a real fingerprint. Amazing. Very impressive. It was a masterpiece of confectionery and no doubt about it.

Okay. He'd have to touch it now. As soon as he touched it, he'd know if it was real or not. If it was marzipan, he could break a bit off. He'd try a nibble, just to see. But if it wouldn't break off . . .

He touched the finger. It felt cold, clammy. He picked it up. He looked at the end that normally would have been attached to a hand. Hmm. It was a clean cut. Just looked a bit like the end of a stick of candy. It was a great fake.

He held the finger between his two hands and went to break a little taste off.

He felt resistance. The stiff resistance of something like . . . bone. This wasn't sugar; this wasn't marzipan. He dropped the finger back onto the desk.

He felt suddenly ill.

"It's real," Fergal whispered. "It's real. It's flesh and blood — real. It's someone's finger!" He moved away from it, pushing his chair back across the bedroom floor.

"What am I going to do? What am I going to do?"

But before he could decide, there was the sound of footsteps coming up the stairs, and his mother's voice calling, "Fergal? Fergal? Are you there? Are you in your room?"

His mother would be there any second. She'd walk right in, probably without even knocking. What was he going to say to her? How could he possibly explain? About what he had there, lying on his desk.

Someone else's finger.

"Fergal! Fergal!"

He didn't want to touch it again, but he had no choice. Fergal picked up the finger by the knuckle and threw it into the desk drawer. He recoiled, and wiped his own fingers over his jeans, as if wiping the finger away.

"Fergal! Fergal!"

"Yes, Mum?"

The door opened.

"Yes, Mum?"

He tried to look innocent. Come to that, he was innocent. He hadn't been responsible for chopping a finger off and putting it in the can. All he had done was to find it.

His mother stared at the empty can and the can opener on his desk.

"What are you doing?"

"Er . . . nothing."

"You haven't opened one of your cans? In your bedroom?"

"Er . . . no . . . that is . . . maybe, just a little bit."

"For heaven's sake, Fergal! You could have had stuff everywhere. At least open them in the kitchen."

"Yes, Mum. Sorry."

"You can't open cans in your bedroom. We don't want baked beans or rice pudding all over your desk, do we?"

"No, Mum."

"So what was in it?"

Fergal tried to look blank.

"In it?"

"The can?"

She was advancing toward the desk now, about to pick the can up to see for herself. She was still wearing her gardening gloves. Inside the dark red of the rubber were her fingers. All ten of them, or eight plus two thumbs, if you wanted to count it that way. But somebody, somewhere, was missing a finger; their finger had ended up in a can. Or maybe all their fingers had ended up in cans. Maybe there was a whole selection of them, a new line of canned fingers.

"It's empty."

"There wasn't really anything to eat in it," Fergal explained. (That wasn't a lie, was it? A half-truth at worst.)

"Nothing?"

"That's why I opened it up here. It felt so light."

Fergal's mother inspected the empty can.

"Well, well," she said. "Fancy that. Not much of a bargain that, then was it, Fergal? A can with nothing in it."

"No, I suppose not. Did you want something, Mum?"

"Yes, I came up to ask if you had any spare batteries. The ones in my radio have gone."

Fergal felt suddenly relieved.

"Yes, I think I have," he said. "They're here in the . . ."

In the drawer.

Why had he said it? Why hadn't he said no?

His mother stood, waiting for him to open the drawer.

And as soon as he opened it, she would see it — the finger, lying there.

She waited. He didn't move.

"Come on, Fergal. Aren't you going to open it? Can I have some batteries? I'll replace them. I'll buy you some new ones next time I go to the supermarket."

Fergal flinched at her mention of the place. He had developed a sudden aversion to supermarkets. They sold canned fingers there. They catered to cannibals.

He reached for the handle of the drawer. There was no way out of it. Was there?

"Actually, I'm not so sure I have any spare batteries. I might have used them up. Here, Mum, have my radio."

"Oh. Are you sure?"

"Positive."

"Won't you want to listen to it?"

"No, no. I'm okay. I've got my iPod."

"Well, if you're sure."

He handed her the radio.

"There you go, Mum."

"Thanks. And if you're going to open any more cans . . ."

"Do it in the kitchen."

"That's right."

"Okay."

The door closed behind her. He heard the sound of the radio as his mother turned it on and retuned it to a classical station. The music faded as she went on down the stairs.

He waited until he heard the back door close, then he pulled the drawer open. There it was, lying there, the finger. He didn't want to touch it again if he could possibly avoid it, so he rummaged around until he found his tweezers and a small plastic bag which had once held his collection of dead wood lice. He picked the finger up with the tweezers and dropped it on top of the paper on his desk, next to the can. He prodded the finger with the points of the tweezers, carefully, as if he half expected it to suddenly come alive and attack him.

Though quite how a solitary, cold, dead finger could attack you, he didn't know. It could hardly strangle you. Poke you in the eye, maybe, or stick itself in your ear, or ram itself up your nose. But nothing fatal.

Fergal turned it over with the tweezers, wondering which finger it was — index finger, ring finger, little finger, the other one, which didn't really have a name — did it? Middle finger, maybe. Was that it?

He put his own hand flat against the desk, as near to the finger as he dared, so as to have something to compare it with.

Yes. From the look of it, it was a little finger. It was bigger than his own little finger, but it could have been an adult's one, he guessed. Whether it had belonged to a man or to a woman, he didn't know. He guessed a man, but he couldn't be certain. There wasn't any nail varnish on it, and it certainly hadn't had any manicures recently involving emery boards or clippers. Nor did it look all that well acquainted with soap and water.

How had it ended up in a can?

Had some horrible crime been committed? And if so, he ought to tell somebody, but who? His mother, his father, the police? Was the finger just the tip of the iceberg? Was there a whole body involved? Chopped up into tiny pieces and put into cans? Fergal felt queasy as his imagination took over. Were there nine other canned fingers somewhere? Ten canned toes? Two canned eyeballs? Two canned ears? One canned nose? Two canned feet (in big cans)? A canned bottom, in a big catering-size can, the sort you found in canteens and restaurant kitchens? Were there two canned knees somewhere, and a selection of canned teeth, all rattling and clattering about?

He somehow couldn't see himself going to the police station to report the discovery of a finger in a can. Well, he could see himself doing it; he just couldn't see himself being believed.

"Excuse me, officer, I'm sorry to trouble you, but I've found this finger, in a can . . ."

"Where did you really get this finger, son? You can tell us now. You won't get into any trouble. The truth is best, son. Now, let's start from the beginning. Whose finger is it, and where, why and when did you cut it off, and what did you do with the rest of the body?"

"But I didn't do anything, officer."

"Now, come along, son. We know you did it, so you may as well confess. We've had our eye on you for some time now. We

know all about you and your activities. Been acting a bit strangely recently, haven't you, lad? In fact, you've always been a bit strange, have you not? A bit on the quirky side. In fact, aren't you the boy who collects the cans? A bit too clever for his own good. There's only a short step, you know, between being clever and becoming a criminal genius."

No, that would never do. He couldn't just take it to the police station, not just like that, not until he knew a bit more about it. If only he had some sort of theory to take along with him . . . but he didn't.

Take it back to the supermarket, then?

No. Just as bad as the police station.

"Excuse me, I'd like a refund, please. I bought this can from you recently, an unlabeled one from the bargain basket, and when I got it home and opened it there was a finger inside —"

"No, you didn't. You couldn't have bought that here! We have a strict no-fingers policy in this supermarket."

They'd deny everything, wouldn't they? Of course they would. Even if he showed them the receipt, they'd still deny it. What supermarket wanted a reputation for selling cans with people's body parts inside? If news of a thing like that got out, the customers would stay away in droves. The only customers they'd have would be cannibals and zombies and fully paid-up members of the living dead.

"You'll eat anything when you're hungry, Fergal, you'd be surprised," his father had said to him one mealtime, when he had been reluctant to tackle his Brussels sprouts.

But Fergal doubted it. He looked at the finger and doubted it very strongly indeed.

If only he had somebody to share the finger with. It wouldn't be so bad, then. How did the saying go again? A problem shared was a problem solved, or a problem halved, anyway — one or the other. What was true of problems could be true of fingers, too; a finger shared was a finger halved. But Fergal could think of nobody he could share the finger with. He wanted someone who would stay calm and not get hysterical, someone who would not be repelled or disgusted. He didn't want an adult who would be bound to get worked up about it and exclaim, "A boy of your age! With a finger in a can! This could do untold psychological damage! It could ruin your life. Quick, ring up a social worker immediately."

No, what Fergal wanted more than anything was somebody like himself. Someone who would take the finger at face value and want, more than anything, to get to the bottom of it.

But, as always, there was no one. Only him.

Fergal steeled himself, picked the finger up with the tweezers, and dropped it into the plastic bag.

Now what? Where could he hide it until he could think what to do next?

Under the bed? In the wardrobe? In the drawer with the earring? In the closet? No. It would rot away and start to smell, and then his mother would be asking questions when she found a moldy old finger in a plastic bag, slowly turning green in the closet.

The freezer. That was it. The freezer in the garage. Nobody would find it in there, not if he put it in down at the very bottom, well hidden under the stacks of frozen vegetables and the frozen french fries and pizzas and all the rest. It could lay there undisturbed for years.

Fergal sealed the plastic bag with tape and put a sticker on the bag, upon which he wrote the date and the letters S. F. F. I. C., which was short for Someone's Finger Found In Can. He took the finger and went downstairs with it. Then, after checking that his mum wasn't about, he made his way to the garage. He lifted the lid of the freezer, took out a stack of burgers, and put the finger at the very bottom, hidden under the base of one of the freezer baskets, then he replaced everything as he had found it.

That would do it. Nobody would know. It was too well hidden.

He closed the lid of the freezer, left the garage, and went back up to his room. Now that the finger was no longer on view, he felt a sense of cold detachment. It was time to look at things logically.

He studied the empty can on his desk, looking for some clue as to where it might have come from. But the letters and numbers printed on the can told him nothing. They were obviously some kind of manufacturer's code, but without the key to it, the characters were meaningless. He decided to keep the empty can anyway, just in case it might yield up some more clues in the future. He put it up on the shelf with his other cans. He picked up and shook every single one, all forty-nine of them, but they were all heavy and full. He compared their codes with the code on the can that had contained the finger. But they were all different. There was neither pattern nor consistency.

Fergal decided to go out on his bicycle for a while to clear his thoughts. He rode up and down the street, thinking about the finger. Whose was it? How had it ever come to be separated from the hand it belonged to? And how — most puzzling of all — had it ever ended up in a can? There had to be an answer. And he wanted to know what it was. For no matter how strange, mysterious, and supernatural a thing may seem, there was always a rational explanation.

It was the same with magic tricks — sawing ladies in half and making elephants disappear. You didn't know how it was done, but you knew that the magician was only human, the same as you. He hadn't really sawed the lady in half, or turned the elephant into a pile of dust. He wasn't a wizard with extraordinary powers, he was just a man who knew how tricks were done and how to present illusion as reality. He distracted your attention. His skill deceived your senses. He made you see what he wanted you to see, and ignore what he didn't.

Distraction, distortion, smoke and mirrors. But there was always a rational, logical explanation. There *was*; there had to be. And fingers and earrings in cans were the same. There was a cogent, rational explanation of how they came to be there. The gold stud could have simply fallen from the ear of someone working on the production line. But the finger, the finger . . .

There had to be an explanation.

Only what?

PART 2

Diary of F. Bamfield. Month of June. Still private.

No nosy parkers to read this.

If you are reading this and you are not F. Bamfield, then you are a nosy parker. So stop reading now. Or you will catch a horrible disease.

June 30

Dear Diary,

I know I haven't filled you in since March, but so much has happened that I couldn't begin to make up lost ground as I would have to write a book, never mind a diary.

You wouldn't believe what has happened to me lately. I have been finding body parts in my cans and they have started off the nightmares again. I had another one last night, where I dreamed I opened this big can up and there was a human head in there and it looked up at me and opened its mouth and said, "I don't suppose you'd have a spare toothbrush by any chance, would you?"

Then it smiled at me and I saw that it didn't have teeth.

I used to think my life was boring, but it's not anymore.

The only trouble is, I don't know if I can handle all the stress.

7. ON THE OTHER HAND

Having somebody's finger in the freezer didn't make as much difference to life as Fergal might have expected. It was probably like having a body buried under the patio. The deed was done, the body was out of sight, and life went on as it always did. You still had to eat your dinner and wash your face and get up and go to school in the morning. And maybe it was lurking there in the back of your mind, but nobody would have known from looking at you that you had such a ghastly and terrible secret.

Fergal thought about the finger a lot. He would find himself doodling in class absentmindedly while the teacher talked. When he looked to see what he had drawn, it would invariably be a finger — well, that or a small gold stud.

A thousand explanations came into his mind, and none of them was satisfactory. Almost as soon as he had formulated a theory, he had rejected it as implausible or inadequate. Yet there was an answer, he knew there was.

If only he could put . . . well . . . his finger on it.

He found himself keeping an eye out for people who might be missing a finger: people in shops, people in the street, everywhere. He was especially interested in anyone who worked with sharp implements. He watched through the window of the local butcher's shop as Mr. Taylor turned carcasses into chops or cut up steaks, wielding knives and cleavers with professional ease.

It would be all too easy to lose a finger in a job like that. All it would need was a moment's inattention . . . and slice! It would be gone, wrapped up with the sausages or fallen into the mincer. Yes, accidentally chopping your finger off would be all too easy. But for it to end up in a can, that was another matter.

One weekend Fergal's parents had someone come round with a chain saw to trim the upper branches of the oak tree in their garden. His father had become worried that its overhanging branches might start to annoy the neighbors or, worse, the oak's spreading roots could undermine the foundation of the house.

Fergal watched from his bedroom window, thinking that here was an exacting and a dangerous job. When the work was done and the man came down the ladder to drink the cup of tea that Fergal's mother had made for him, Fergal saw, when he removed his protective gloves, that he had a finger missing. On his left hand. His little finger.

Fergal couldn't help but stare at where the finger had once been. He was even tempted to go and get the finger he had found out of the freezer, to show it to the man and ask, as casually as possible, "I wonder if this would happen to be yours?" Maybe it could even be sewn back on by some expert surgeon, if it wasn't too late. It might be worth a try.

But somehow he couldn't do it. And so the finger remained where it was, in the bottom of the freezer in the garage, out of sight, but forever in Fergal's mind.

***

Weeks went by.

As a matter of habit, Fergal continued to rummage through the bargain basket in the supermarket when he went with his mother to do the week's shopping.

Finally, one Saturday morning, his diligence was rewarded.

Immediately on entering the shop Fergal spotted the silver gleam of a can without a label lying at the top of the bargain bin. It seemed to call to him, to lure him over, almost as if he were a can himself and the can some powerful magnet, its attraction irresistible.

He knew instinctively, before he even reached out for it, that this can was going to be a special one. There was something about it, it had an aura, a look. There was going to be an answer in here, or if not an answer, at least a clue of some kind. Whatever was inside this can, it was going to draw him closer to the ultimate solution. He just needed to pick it up, take it to the checkout, pay for it, take it home, open it up and . . .

"Excuse me! That's *mine!*"

Another hand landed upon the can just as his own closed around it.

"What?"

Startled, Fergal looked up to find himself staring into two brown eyes, which peered at him from behind a pair of spectacles. Above the spectacles, an unkempt mass of brown hair stuck out in all directions, as if trying to make a break for freedom from the hairband, which attempted (with minimal success) to contain it.

It was a girl. A bit of an awkward, lumpy-looking one too. The kind who probably went around tripping over her own feet, spilling drinks, crashing into furniture, and bringing down the curtains. She looked like the kind of girl who always had two or three Band-Aids attached to her knees, her shins, or her elbows. She looked like the kind of girl whose parents would be anxious to keep her away from sharp knives.

She looked a bit assertive too.

"I'm afraid that can is *mine*! As in, *it belongs to me*!"

Fergal kept hold of his end. He wasn't going to lose out. Not to a girl.

"It's mine," he said. "I got it first."

"You did not," the girl told him. "I got hold of it long before you did."

"You didn't!"

"Did so!"

"Did not!"

The girl tried to wrestle the can away from him, but Fergal stood his ground. He in turn tried to pry it away from her, but she had as firm and as strong a grip as he did.

"Let go," the girl said. "That can is mine by rights."

"What rights?"

"I saw it first."

"No, you didn't."

"How do you know?"

"How do *you*?"

"I just do."

"Well, so do I!"

It was a deadlock. They both stood there, like two tug-of-war teams on either side of a rope, equally matched, perfectly balanced, and neither able to get the advantage.

"Let go!"

"You let go!"

Fergal took a good look at her. She looked a bit intelligent to him. Yes, she definitely seemed like one of those girls whom people watched for a while and then said, "Hmm, she seems clever," and they hoped she was, for her sake, because otherwise she was in trouble, as she was somewhat lacking in the charm department.

"Look," the girl said, "I saw this can first and it belongs to me. Not only that, it's more important to me than it is to you, so there."

Fergal kept hold of his share of the can, unpersuaded by these statements.

"How do you know," he said, "that it's more important to you?"

"Because I need it," the girl said. "For my collection!"

Fergal almost let go of the can then. Almost, but not quite. His heart beat faster. He stared at the girl, wondering if he had heard her correctly, hoping in some ways that he had, and in other ways that he hadn't.

"Your collection?"

"That was what I said, didn't I?"

"You mean . . . you collect cans?"

The girl gave him a defiant look.

"Some reason why I shouldn't?" she said rather defensively.

"N-no," Fergal told her. Then he hesitated before revealing that, "It's just . . . I collect them too."

Her grip on the can momentarily relaxed. His revelation was as much of a surprise to her as hers had been to him. But then her hold tightened again.

"Don't believe you," she said.

"It's true."

"Prove it."

"Why else would I want this can if I didn't collect them?" Her eyes narrowed behind her spectacles. "If you really do collect cans, what do you know about them?"

Fergal hesitated, then said, "I know that you find things in them."

The girl lowered her voice.

"What things?"

"Special things."

"Such as?"

Again Fergal paused. Could he — should he — tell her? Was this finally someone in whom he could confide? Could she be depended on not to laugh or to sneer at him with incredulity and doubt? But you had to trust somebody, and she did seem reliable in her odd, eccentric-looking way. He decided to risk it.

"Things you don't tell your parents about," he said. "Things you wouldn't expect to find in cans. Secret things . . . spooky things."

The girl looked at him intently through her glasses.

"Spooky things?"

"Yes."

"And creepy ones?"

Fergal nodded.

"Hmm."

The girl seemed willing to give him the benefit of the doubt.

"Okay," she said. "Tell you what — let's share this can between us."

"Share it? How?"

"We pay half each and we both own the can . . . and whatever's inside. We take turns with it, a week each."

It seemed fair enough by the sound of it, and yet . . .

"Who gets the can first?" Fergal said. "Me or you?"

"I do. I get it first for a week. And then you get it for a week."

"And how do I do that?"

"Well . . . you can come round to my house if you like, and pick it up."

Fergal still held back. He'd never been invited round to anyone's house before, let alone a strange girl's.

"I don't even know where you live," he said. "Where do you live?"

"Not far. Where do you live?"

"Not far either."

"That's all right then."

"Are you sure you live round here? I've never seen you at our school," Fergal said suspiciously.

"That's probably because I don't go to your school. I've never seen you at *my* school, come to that."

"Where do you go?"

"St. Helen's."

"That's a girls' school."

"That's probably why I've not seen you there, then."

"Could be."

Fergal held tightly on to the can a moment longer, then he let it go.

"Okay," he said. "I trust you." He didn't normally trust girls, but in the case of a fellow can collector, he was prepared to make an exception.

"Okay," the girl said. "I trust you too."

She shook the can. It rattled.

"It *is* a special one!" Fergal said.

She nodded and handed the can over to him.

"See for yourself."

He felt the weight of the can. It was very light, the lightest yet. He shook it. The rattle was faint, hardly a rattle at all.

"How many have you found like this?" he asked, lowering his voice to a whisper so that other shoppers wouldn't overhear.

"Two," she said. "You?"

"Two," Fergal told her. "The same."

"What was in them?" the girl asked. "The cans you found?"

Fergal felt reluctant to tell her. She might well be a genuine fellow collector, but there was such a thing as professional rivalry. You didn't want to give all your secrets away, at least not without the guarantee of getting one back in return.

"Something nice and something nasty," he said. "What about you?"

"Same here," she told him. "Something nice and something nasty . . . or maybe a better word might be . . . weird."

"Tell me one of your things and I'll tell you one of mine."

"All right then, I'll tell you one. The first thing I found was —"

But she didn't get a chance to say. They were interrupted by Fergal's mother bearing down upon them with her trolley.

"Fergal, *there* you are! I've been looking for you everywhere. I might have known I'd find you here by the bargain basket. Oh . . . have you made a friend?"

And just as Fergal's mother descended upon him, another woman, who by the look of her sticky-out hair and glasses had to be the girl's mother, arrived at the bargain basket too, her trolley as laden to overflowing as Fergal's mother's.

"Charlotte! There you are! Whatever are you doing? I told you to meet me by the boxes of cookies at least ten minutes ago and . . . Oh . . . is this someone you know?"

Fergal looked at Charlotte; she looked at him. They knew each other's names now, without the embarrassment of introductions.

"I'm sorry, is this your daughter?"

"Is this your son?"

Fergal's heart sank to the bottom of his sneakers. His mother didn't even know this lady, but that didn't mean they weren't in for a good long natter.

"This is Fergal."

"This is Charlotte."

"And what school does she go to?"

"St. Helen's."

"Oh, Fergal's just around the corner. You live locally?"

"Just moved here a few months ago."

"Oh, how nice. And does Charlotte have a lot of friends?"

"Yes and no. Not that many." There was a conspiratorial lowering of voices. "She's a little bit . . . individual."

"Fergal too."

"Has her own interests."

"Fergal as well."

Fergal and Charlotte stood awkwardly by while their mothers discussed them, looking rather like two cattle whose relative merits were being debated by a couple of thick-skinned farmers at a county fair. Fergal wondered if his mother might prod him in a minute, to draw attention to his better features, or possibly to his fat bits.

"She's thought to be highly intelligent," Charlotte's mother went on, nodding in her daughter's direction, as if she might win a coveted rosette for Best in Show.

"Fergal's said to be very clever too," Fergal's mother said, not to be outdone.

"Not in an exam-passing way," Charlotte's mother hastily added, lest she be asked to produce evidence of results.

"No, nor Fergal exactly."

"More . . . just intelligent."

"Yes."

"In an individual way."

The two mothers smiled at each other. If Fergal was glad to have met a fellow can collector, his mother was equally pleased at having met somebody with whom to share her concerns over her offspring.

The two women adjourned to a corner where their trolleys wouldn't block the aisle.

"You know, to be frank, Fergal does have some rather unusual hobbies."

"Charlotte too."

"He collects cans, you know."

"Cans? Well, that is interesting. Charlotte has quite a collection herself. It all started about . . ."

On they went, wrapped up in their conversation. Their voices turned to drones. They had soon completely forgotten about the presence of the very children they were talking about.

Charlotte took the opportunity to shake the can again; then she passed it over to Fergal to shake and to listen to as well.

"What do you think?" she said.

"Interesting," he nodded.

"Can't wait to get the opener to it," she said.

"Me neither."

"Shall I come round to your house or you come round to mine?"

"Don't mind. Whatever."

"You come round to mine then. And we'll open it together."

"All right."

"And bring your best cans."

"I've already opened the best ones."

"Bring what you found inside them, then."

Fergal felt that before he did anything like that, he ought to warn this girl what she was in for. Some girls were a bit delicate, as far as Fergal knew. They might not be too keen on the idea of canned fingers.

"One of the things I found is a bit gruesome," he told her.

"Fine by me."

If some girls were delicate, Charlotte plainly was not one of the overly sensitive variety.

"The more gruesome the better," she said. "Bring it along. I've got some gruesome stuff myself, as a matter of fact."

Fergal looked at her curiously, convinced that whatever her find was, it couldn't possibly be as gruesome as his.

"How gruesome?" he said.

"Pretty gruesome," Charlotte said.

"Where do you keep it?" Fergal asked.

"In the freezer," she said, and their eyes met, with mute, but mutual understanding.

Fergal nodded slowly. "I wouldn't mind seeing that."

"Tomorrow?" Charlotte said.

"Sunday? Okay. I'll just have to think of a way . . ."

But it turned out not to be necessary. Deceit and deviousness weren't needed. Their mothers were already getting them organized and making their arrangements for them.

"Charlotte, dear . . ."

"Fergal . . ."

"I was talking to Fergal's mother here . . ."

"We only just met, but Charlotte's mother here tells me . . ."

"And we were thinking . . ."

"That it might be a good idea . . ."

But Charlotte interrupted them.

"Mum, can Fergal come round tomorrow?"

It stopped them in their tracks.

"Oh, yes, well, I'm sure he can if that's all right with his mother."

"It's fine by me. It'll be nice for you to get out of the house for a while, won't it, Fergal, instead of moping about on your own in your bedroom and poring over your . . . cans."

"Oh yes, the cans. Charlotte's interested in cans, aren't you, dear?"

The two mothers plainly hoped that if they got their offspring together, their friendship might prove a distraction from the dreaded things. And if that didn't work, well, at least they would all be in the same boat together. It wasn't so bad to have a weirdo in the family when you found that other families had one too. There was strength and comfort in numbers.

So it was arranged that Fergal would go round to Charlotte's house the next day. And it was quietly agreed between Fergal and Charlotte, as soon as their mothers were out of earshot, that Fergal would bring with him the contents of his best cans. Then they would compare and contrast what they had both found, and possibly begin together to make sense of what they couldn't make sense of alone.

Fergal handed over half the cost of the new can to Charlotte, and she paid for it at the checkout.

"But no opening it," he reminded her. "Not until I'm there as well."

"No need to worry," Charlotte said. "You can trust me."

He hoped he could. He really did hope so. After all, if you couldn't trust a fellow collector of cans, whom could you trust?

8. CLOSE YOUR EYES

"What are you doing, Fergal?"

"Nothing."

His mother was calling him from inside the house.

"What are you doing in the garage?"

"Nothing. Just . . . admiring the lawn mower. That is . . . getting my shoes."

The impatience in her tone rose a level.

"We're going to be late, Fergal!"

Never mind that. Where was it? Where was his finger?

"Are you ready, Fergal?"

"Almost."

"And what does 'almost' mean?"

It was obvious what it meant, wasn't it? Almost meant almost — nearly, practically . . . only where was that finger? He was sure he had left it there, at the bottom of the freezer, under all the burgers and the pizzas, wrapped in its own plastic bag.

"Fergal, I won't tell you again," she told him again. "We're going to be late. What are you doing in there?"

"Nothing."

"Well it's taking you long enough."

"Just a minute!"

He took all the pizzas out and dumped them on the garage floor.

"Fergal!"

He felt harassed and put-upon. Why did she have to take him anyway? It turned out that Charlotte only lived a mile or so away. Why couldn't he have walked round on his own?

"Fergal!"

Her voice came from the kitchen, louder still. But where was his finger?

"Fergal!"

She was coming. The voice was getting nearer.

He found it. It had rolled under one of the other wire baskets in the freezer, not the one he had left it under. It must have shifted when someone had slammed the freezer lid. He grabbed it and stuffed it into his pocket just before she walked in.

"Fergal, whatever are you doing in the freezer?"

"Who, me?"

"There's no one else here. And why have you got all the pizzas out?"

Fergal looked at the pizzas stacked up on the garage floor and wondered what to say.

"I thought I'd take one with me," he said.

His mother stared at him.

"What?"

"I thought I'd take a pizza with me, round to Charlotte's."

"A pizza? A frozen pizza?"

"Yes."

"Why?"

"As a sort of . . . you know . . . in case we got hungry . . . or in case they asked me to stay to tea, and didn't have enough food to go round."

"Fergal, I hardly think that when you go to visit people that you need to turn up with a frozen pizza."

"Well, shall I take them some french fries instead?" he asked innocently.

"No! Certainly not!" his mother snapped.

"It was only a thought," he said.

"Maybe so. But put them all back in the freezer and let us go. Now come on."

"I could walk round on my own," he offered.

"No, it's all right. I can give you a lift."

Fergal suspected the truth was that his mother wanted to see Charlotte's mother again and discuss in greater detail the problems of having clever offspring who collect cans.

So they got into the car and drove off.

Fergal worried about the finger as they went. It would be starting to thaw now, to defrost. "Defrosted finger"— it sounded very odd. His pocket would start to get damp and the finger would become softer, more malleable. It might even bend at its joints as he walked.

Eeuch.

In Fergal's other pocket was the little gold stud. In the small rucksack beside him were his outdoor coat, his mobile phone, his Cans

Book, and the actual can in which he had discovered the finger. It was as well to have all the necessary information with him. It was a pity, he felt in retrospect, that he had thrown away the can that had contained the gold earring, his first real "find."

He wondered about this girl, Charlotte. He didn't normally make friends with girls, or with anyone, really. But the exceptional circumstances demanded it. The normal hostilities between boys and girls of their age would have to be suspended if they were to get to the bottom of it all.

The car pulled up outside Charlotte's house. It looked very much like their own, in a similar street of semidetached houses with leafy gardens. They went to the door, and as he had suspected would happen, Charlotte's mother invited his own mother in for coffee and a chat while he was taken up to Charlotte's room.

Charlotte's room was a bit like her hair — no matter how she tried to tidy it and to keep it under control, ten minutes later it was wild again. Charlotte Pettigrew's collection of cans occupied one whole bookcase.

It wasn't exactly like Fergal's, for she collected cans with labels as well as cans without. Some of them looked ancient, maybe fifty or a hundred years old, Fergal reckoned, going by their faded, old-fashioned designs.

Charlotte didn't stand on ceremony or bother with any polite small talk or meaningless chitchat.

"Well," she said, "did you bring your stuff?"

Fergal nodded.

"These your cans?" he said.

"Obviously," Charlotte said.

"They've got labels."

"Some of them. I get them in junk shops and charity shops and places like that, and people give them to me for presents. They're quite expensive, some of them. See that one there . . ."

She pointed to a can with an old-fashioned red-and-white label reading CORNED BEEF.

"What about it?"

"Cost fifty pounds."

"Never."

"Did so."

"You paid fifty pounds for a can?"

"Not me. My uncle. It was a birthday present. *Some* cans are worth hundreds — thousands even. If you get a can that, say, had been on a polar expedition, and had maybe once belonged to Scott of the Antarctic, or Marco Polo, or somebody like that, you could name your own price."

Fergal looked at her dubiously.

"I didn't think they had cans of corned beef when Marco Polo was alive."

"No, they probably didn't," Charlotte agreed. "But that was just an example. So where's your stuff, then?"

Fergal felt in his pocket. His grip tightened around the now slightly soggy finger in the plastic bag.

"Where's your stuff first?" he said.

"In the drawer," Charlotte said.

"And where's the can from the bargain basket?"

"Here," Charlotte said.

And there it was, sitting on the windowsill, still unopened, just as she had promised, and beside it was a can opener.

"Well? What shall we do? Compare stuff first, or open the can?"

Fergal hesitated, then said, "Compare stuff."

"Gruesome first, or not so gruesome?"

"Not so gruesome, then gruesome."

"Okay. You going first?"

"All right. Here. This is the first thing I found."

Fergal took the small gold earring from his pocket and placed it down on Charlotte's dressing table.

"It's a sleeper."

"That's right."

"Interesting."

"What did you find first?"

"This." Charlotte reached into her desk drawer, took something out and placed it next to the gold stud.

"It's a ring."

"That's right."

"Can I touch it?"

"Go ahead. Pick it up if you like."

"There's initials on it."

"It's a signet ring."

"What does that mean?"

"Don't you know?"

"I'm not well up on rings."

"A signet ring is a ring which has the initials of the owner etched into it."

"What for? In case he forgets his name?"

"How do you know it's a he?"

"Anyone, then."

"I don't know, it's just for decoration. It's hardly going to be because you keep forgetting your name, is it?"

"I don't know. What are the letters?"

"J.D.S."

"Interesting."

"That's what I thought."

"Looks like gold too. Like my ear stud."

"It is gold. My mum said."

"You showed it to her, then?"

"Well, I must have done or how could she have said."

"You're pretty stroppy for a girl, aren't you?" Fergal said.

"Any reason why girls shouldn't be stroppy — not that I am stroppy, but if I was, is there any reason why I shouldn't be?"

Fergal thought about it.

"No," he said. "None at all."

"Good. Okay. Show us your gruesome stuff then," Charlotte said.

Fergal reached into his pocket and took out the small, damp package.

"Close your eyes."

"Don't be stupid."

"If you close your eyes, then when you open them, you can see it all at once."

"Oh, all right, then."

"I'll put it on the desk."

Fergal didn't want to put the thawing finger down on the bed. It might leave a mark on the duvet.

Charlotte closed her eyes.

"No peeking."

"Get on with it."

He unwrapped and extracted the finger, put the plastic bag down on the desk, and set the finger on top of it. He no longer felt so squeamish in dealing with dead and squishy body parts. At this rate, he could even end up as an undertaker, or a professional embalmer, or possibly a brain surgeon. "All right. You can open them now."

She did.

"Oh, wicked! Oh, gruesome! That is bad!"

Charlotte exclaimed so loudly that her mother must have heard her, and she called up the stairs.

"What's going on up there? Are you two all right?"

"It's all right, Mum, we're just having . . . a game of cards."

"Well, keep the volume down."

The kitchen door shut again.

Charlotte stared at the finger. Even as a severed digit, it had seen better days. It had a rather gangrenous aspect to it now and it emitted a faint, but distinctly unpleasant, odor. It was slowly going off. Yet, far from repelled by it, she seemed fascinated, enthralled.

"Wow! Cool!" she said. "When you said you had gruesome stuff,

I never thought you meant anything like this. This is gruesome. This is gruesome and a half. Wow!"

Without asking permission, she picked the finger up and held it to the light.

"Hmm . . ." she said.

"What?"

"Nothing. I could be wrong."

"Wrong about what?"

"Look at it."

"Where?"

"There. Near the bottom, where it got cut off."

"What about it?"

"There's a mark, all the way around it."

"I know. I saw that. What is it?"

"Well, it could have been caused by whatever cut the finger off . . . or it could be the mark left by something else."

"Like?"

"Like a ring?"

She turned the finger around in her hands. She looked at the dead but warming digit from all angles, then laid it back down on the plastic bag.

"All right," Fergal said. "So where's your gruesome stuff? Supposing you actually have any gruesome stuff."

"Oh, I've got gruesome stuff, don't you worry," Charlotte said. "I've got gruesome as good as you. Possibly even better."

"I doubt it."

"Well, there's one way to find out."

"That's right. So let's see it, then."

"Okay. You asked for it. But you'd better not faint or pass out."

"I'm a boy."

She gave him a cool, appraising look, as if to say, "So what? You think that makes a difference?"

"So where is it?" Fergal asked.

"Right here."

Charlotte took a small tin from a drawer, an old extra-strong-mint tin with a lift-up lid. It had a slight covering of what could have been perspiration.

"I've been keeping it in the freezer too," she said. "It might not have totally thawed out yet."

"All the same to me."

There was a small potted cactus on her desk, sitting on a saucer. Charlotte took the saucer from under the pot and placed it in readiness to receive the contents of the can.

"Close your eyes, then, like I did."

Fergal closed his eyes. He heard the sound of the tin being opened. He heard the lid being placed on the desk. Then he heard a slow, slithering sound, as something slid from the can into Charlotte's hand, and was then placed — he surmised — upon the saucer. "Okay. You can open them now."

Fergal's eyes opened wide — and instantly got wider. "Oh, wow!"

"See, I told you."

"That is gruesome."

"Isn't it?"

"It looks so real."

"It is real," Charlotte snapped.

"Oh, grisly! Gross!"

"Totally, double gross!" she agreed, with a certain pride in her voice.

"That's as good as my finger. Or as bad as my finger."

"It's worse than your finger."

"I wouldn't say that."

"I would. Well, aren't you going to pick it up, then?"

"Is it all right to pick it up?"

"Yes. If you're not afraid to."

"I'm not afraid."

"So pick it up."

"All right, I will." He reached out and touched it. It was still cold. Cold and brittle, gradually turning clammy and moist. He picked it up by the lobe and placed it flat upon the palm of his other hand.

It was an ear. A human ear. With a tiny hole in it. For an earring.

"It's an ear," he said. "Off someone's head."

Fergal looked from the ear to Charlotte, to the finger slowly thawing out on top of the small plastic bag.

"You don't think . . ." he began. But then his mouth seemed suddenly dry. "You don't think," he began again, "that perhaps somebody has been . . . murdered."

Charlotte looked out at him from behind her stack of sticking-out-everywhere hair. "I think it's a possibility," she said, "that we can't altogether rule out."

9. DID HE FALL, OR WAS HE PUSHED?

For a time, neither of them spoke. Fergal and Charlotte sat and contemplated the objects on the desk in Charlotte's room: the ring, the stud, the thawing ear, the finger, slowly coming back to life — or to death, rather — as they warmed up in the heat of the room.

"Do you think . . . ?" Fergal began.

"Think what?"

"That it all belongs to the same person?"

"Might do," Charlotte said. "Maybe it does. How would you know?"

"That mark," Fergal said. "Around the finger. As if there'd been a ring on it once . . ."

Charlotte pushed the ring toward him.

"Try it," she said. "See if it fits."

Fergal had been hoping that *she* would put the ring upon the finger to see if it fitted, which was why he had made the suggestion in the first place. But she hadn't taken the hint in quite the way he had intended.

He reached out and took the finger in his left hand and the ring in his right. He slid the ring over the top of the finger, just like someone who was getting married — getting betrothed . . . to a finger.

"*Do you, Fergal Bamfield, take this finger to be your lawfully wedded . . . well . . . extra finger?*"

No. He did not!

"Well?"

Fergal held up the finger for Charlotte to see. The ring fitted perfectly around it. They could have been made for each other, to have and to hold, until . . . well . . . death did them part.

"Wow!" she said. "What about the ear stud . . . and the ear?"

Fergal didn't offer. He'd done his bit. It was Charlotte's turn to do hers.

She didn't flinch. She picked up the severed ear and inserted the sleeper into the lobe.

"Fits," she said. "But then, wouldn't it anyway? A hole in an ear is a hole in an ear. Earrings all come in standard sizes. It doesn't exactly prove . . ."

"No," Fergal agreed, "it doesn't exactly prove . . . but then, when you find an earring in one can, and an actual ear in another . . ."

"Pretty conclusive." Charlotte nodded.

They both turned to look toward the can. The most recent can. The one they had found together in the bargain basket.

"Shall we open it?" Charlotte asked.

Fergal nodded.

"Better had."

She picked up the can opener.

"Shall I do it?"

"If you like."

"Right."

Before she did, she shook the can. The sound seemed less of a rattle now and more of a dull thud, as though whatever was in there had become soft and glutinous, like a small ball of jelly.

"You don't think, do you," Fergal said, "that it's . . . another *bit*?"

"Another bit of *what*?"

"Of the body?"

"If there *is* a body," Charlotte said.

"If there's *not* a body, where have the ear and the finger come from?"

"Might have been an accident, in the packing factory," Charlotte said.

"Maybe," Fergal agreed. "But a finger *and* an ear . . . sounds a bit like a fatal accident to me. Always assuming it was an accident, of course."

Charlotte contemplated the ear and the finger, sitting on the desk, sporting their jewelry.

"I don't suppose we even know for sure that the ear belongs to the finger or that the finger belongs to the ear."

"Well, two accidents involving two different people sounds a bit suspicious," Fergal said.

"It all sounds suspicious."

"Go on. Let me hold the can."

Charlotte passed it to him. He held it to his ear and shook it gently, his face assuming a thoughtful expression, as if the sound alone might reveal what was inside. He thought of his father, with a glass of wine in his hand, and the way he would sniff the wine before drinking.

"You know," Fergal said. "I think we'd better prepare ourselves for the worst."

"Do you mean what I think you mean?" Charlotte said, her face growing pale, her lips pressing together.

Fergal nodded.

"Yes."

"An eyeball?"

"Could be," he said. "Possibly plural."

"Two of them! Double eyeballs?"

"Would you rather I opened it?" he asked, feeling uncharacteristically strong and protective — a sensation which soon evaporated.

"I can manage," Charlotte said a little haughtily. "I'm not afraid of an eyeball."

"Nor me," Fergal asserted. And he wasn't. But two of them, that was a different matter.

They both looked apprehensively at the label-less can.

Charlotte picked up a small ornamental dish, one she had made and painted herself at a pottery shop, during someone's birthday party. It looked a bit girly to Fergal, with its floral design and pink wandering roses.

She tipped the hair clips off it and set the dish under the can.

"Just in case it is an eyeball," she said. "Don't want it going everywhere. There's nothing worse than a couple of squishy eyeballs rolling all over your desk. Can make a terrible mess of your homework, stuff like that."

She pressed the can opener into the rim of the lid.

"Okay," she said, "I'm starting opening now, in case you don't want to look. Whatever's in here might not be suitable for people of a nervous disposition."

"I'm not nervous!" Fergal said nervously.

"Right. Then don't blame me if you faint."

Charlotte squeezed the handles of the can opener together. The cutter bit into the can. There was the faint *whoosh* as the vacuum was breached. Then she turned the butterfly handle. Round the cutter went, biting into the lid.

"Well?"

"Watch."

She took the dish and placed it on top of the can. Then she inverted both can and dish, then took the can away.

There the contents were, sitting on the hand-painted, handmade ceramic surface, naked, exposed — revealed at last. "*Eeuch!*" Fergal said. But it wasn't a true *eeuch*. It was more the kind of *eeuch* people come out with when presented with plates of unwanted vegetables, usually green ones.

"*Eeuch!*"

"Double *eeuch*."

Sitting on the ceramic plate was a large, plump, eyeball-sized . . .

Mushroom.

Fergal and Charlotte looked at it with feelings both of relief and of disappointment. "It's not an eyeball, then?"

Fergal said. "No."

"I was sure it was going to be an eyeball."

"I was expecting an eyeball too," Charlotte said. "I was all psyched up for an eyeball."

"Me too," Fergal said. "Pity."

Then his mother's voice broke the spell of their complete and utter absorption in things in cans.

"Fergal! We'll have to go soon!" Her voice boomed up the stairs.

So she had never even left. She had been down in the kitchen talking to Charlotte's mother all this time. Fergal looked at the clock on Charlotte's desk. A whole two hours had passed.

"Sounds like I'll have to go."

"What do you want to do with your finger? Leave it here?"

Fergal didn't know if he trusted Charlotte with his finger. Leave her his finger? He might never see it again. But then, it might be easier. He wouldn't have to try to smuggle it back into the freezer in the garage.

"Okay," he said finally. "But look after it, won't you?"

"I will. So what are we going to do about everything? Should we go to the police? And tell them we suspect there's been a murder?"

There was a glint in Charlotte's eye as she spoke.

"*Do* we suspect there's been a murder though?" Fergal said. "Maybe it was only an accident in a canning factory."

"If we had a bit more evidence . . ."

"But we don't. At least not yet. But if we kept looking. If we found a few more cans, with a few more, well . . . bits in them. What do you think?"

"Okay." Charlotte nodded. "We'll both keep looking, in bargain baskets everywhere. And as soon as we find anything . . ."

"We ring each other up."

"Right. It's a deal."

Charlotte put her hand out. Fergal shook it.

"Deal."

"Fergal! Time to go!" His mother's voice called up the stairs again.

He turned to Charlotte. "Better go," he said.

"Okay."

"Quick, give me your mobile number and your e-mail."

"Give me yours," Charlotte said. "I'll text mine to you."

"Okay." Fergal scribbled his phone number down.

"Here. And you keep the finger. I'll hang on to the stud."

He prized the stud from the ear and put it into his pocket. Then he hurriedly wrapped the finger in the plastic bag and handed it to her.

"I'll hide it in the freezer with my ear." She smiled.

It almost seemed like a kind of togetherness.

"Fergal, we're going!"

"Right. See you, then."

"Bye then, Fergal."

"Bye . . . er . . . Charlotte."

"This is quite exciting, really, isn't it?" she said, as she saw him downstairs and to the front door. Her mother overheard.

"What's that, dear? What's exciting?"

"Oh . . . just things," Charlotte said. "Bye then, Fergal. See you."

***

Wasn't it strange, Fergal thought to himself on the drive home, how grown-ups always wanted to know your business? But wasn't it equally strange how little of your business you told them if you could get away with it? And finally, wasn't it strange how easily you could get away with it? Because there he was, being driven along, the owner of a dismembered finger. He wondered what his mother would do if he told her all about the finger, if he asked her to drive back to Charlotte's and he showed it to her and said, "Here you are, Mum. This is what Charlotte and I were doing. What do you think?"

What would her reaction be? One of two things, probably. Either she just wouldn't listen at all and would say, "That's nice, dear. Very good. Oh, a finger, yes, very nice."

Or she'd start screaming and have a breakdown and go wacko.

Fergal decided not to say anything, just to be on the safe side. He didn't want his mother going wacko. Things were difficult enough already. And besides, who'd cook the supper?

It was funny how dangerous a finger could be. A finger could do a lot. It could press a button to launch a deadly missile, it could squeeze the trigger of a gun. A finger could be a very dangerous thing indeed.

Even a dead one.

In the wrong hands.

***

"So how did you and Charlotte get on, Fergal?" his mother asked him when they arrived home.

"Fine," he grunted noncommittally.

"Nice to have someone to share your hobby with," his mother said.

"Yes," Fergal agreed.

"Did you arrange to see each other again?"

"Said I might give her a call," Fergal said. "As soon as I had some interesting new cans to talk about."

"Oh, good. I'd better start the tea. Your father should be back soon from his golf."

She busied herself in the kitchen, getting pans and plates out.

"What is for tea, Mum?" Fergal asked.

"Fish fingers all right?" she said.

"Fine," Fergal said. "Shall I get them out of the freezer for you?"

"If you would. You know where they are."

"Okay. I'll find them."

Fergal went to the garage and took the fish fingers out.

Fingers.

There were all kinds of them.

Fish fingers, Butterfingers, green thumbs, ladyfingers, even fingers on the hands of the long arm of the law. It was amazing how many different sorts of fingers there were.

There was an answer to this puzzle of the mysterious things in cans. Fergal knew there was. There had to be.

10. THE MALL

Three long weeks went by. Fergal looked, Charlotte searched, they both kept on hoping. Neither of them could pass a shop without dashing in to see if there was a bargain basket on display and, if so, whether there were any unlabeled cans in it.

But it was Fergal who found it. In a supermarket in the shopping mall on the far side of town. His father had been delegated to take Fergal there in order to buy some new school trousers.

Once they had bought the trousers, Fergal's dad suggested that they take a little look in the golf equipment shop for five minutes. Fergal knew from bitter experience that five minutes in the golf shop invariably turned out to be forty-five minutes in the golf shop, so he pleaded with his father to let him wander round the mall on his own.

"Well, the shops are all enclosed, so I suppose you can't come to much harm. And you've got your mobile, haven't you?"

"Yes, Dad."

"Well, keep it turned on, so I can ring you if I want to."

"Okay, Dad."

"And no buying chocolate bars on the sly."

"No, Dad. And no buying any golf clubs on the sly."

"Sorry? What was that, Fergal? I missed that."

"Nothing, Dad."

"Okay. Just half an hour, then, and I'll meet you back here at the entrance to the golf shop."

"Okay, Dad."

"Right."

"Oh, and Fergal . . ."

"I know, Dad. Don't talk to anyone and don't go off with strangers even if they say that your dad sent them."

"Exactly."

"Okay."

Mr. Bamfield watched his son go, wondering if he was doing the right thing, letting him wander off on his own. He kept watching as Fergal walked on along the concourse of the mall. He felt a pang of sadness, as if Fergal had been deprived of his freedom and a proper childhood by a world in which cars and the fear of strangers were every parent's nightmare.

No. Fergal would be all right, he decided. He had to have a little independence. He was getting older, growing up. He was entitled to a bit of independence, and even a few secrets — as long as they weren't too ghastly.

He turned his back and went on into the golf shop. "Good morning, sir," the salesman said. "And what can we do for you?"

Fergal's dad had the feeling that he might be spending some money.

**

It wasn't always easy to find the bargain basket in supermarkets, especially when they were great, vast barns of places the size of airplane hangars. Sometimes even the assistants didn't know where the bargain basket was, or even if there was a bargain basket.

"Sorry, I only work here at weekends, I'm afraid. I'm at school the rest of the time."

Fergal wondered if, when he got older, he might get a weekend job in a supermarket, filling up the shelves, perhaps. He'd like a job like that. He'd get first pickings then, when it came to cans, and get paid for it as well.

Of course, in some countries children had to work. They never got to go to school; they never had days off or holidays. They just sat and worked, making carpets or shoes, slaves rather than employees. It was a hard life for some children.

"Excuse me, is there a bargain basket here, please?"

Fergal had got fed up with wandering down the aisles and had decided to ask for assistance. He thought that the plump lady in the overalls would be the best person to ask. Her name badge read EUNICE.

"Over there, love, by the sugar. Counting the pennies, are we? Looking for some broken cookies and things like that? Used to do the same myself once, when I was your age. There you go."

Fergal thanked her and went to the bargain basket. But there was nothing of any interest to him, so he went back out into the main concourse of the mall.

He glanced at his watch. He now only had ten minutes left before his allotted thirty minutes of freedom were up. His dad would be ringing him on his mobile soon, saying, "Fergal, where are you? I thought we had an arrangement . . . I thought we'd agreed . . . well, no excuses, you get here now!"

There was time for one more quick search. He hurried along to a small, seedy-looking supermarket. It was plainly in decline, being forced out of business by glossier, gleamier places.

"Excuse me, is there a bargain basket?"

"It's all bargains here, dear."

Fergal must have looked so crestfallen, the lady he had spoken to gave him a smile.

"Most customers would be glad to hear that, dear, not disappointed," she said. Then she pointed him toward the till.

"Over there, love. On your way out."

Fergal made his way to the bargain basket. He rummaged around in it. This supermarket didn't seem to sell many ordinary brands. They were all unknown to him. They had names like Nebbeck's Nutty Spread, or Kollenpecker's Krispy Kornflakes, but the box had been made to look very similar to the more famous cornflakes Fergal had at home.

As he rummaged through, he realized that he was not alone. Other bargain hunters were also at work — two elderly ladies and a man with a drop on the end of his nose.

Fergal saw, to his dismay, that one of the old ladies was clutching a can — a can without a label.

But she didn't want it. She had only picked it up out of the basket in order to criticize it to her friend.

"Look at that. No label. Whatever next? I never buy them with no labels. You don't know what's in them. A bargain's not a bargain if you've got no use for it. It's just a waste of money. And anyway, it feels like it's empty, this one. Feels like there's hardly anything in it. Just half a pea or something."

She dropped the can back into the bargain basket. It made a hollow, empty clank.

Fergal grabbed the can before anyone else could. The man with the drop on the end of his nose was also looking at the can with curiosity, but his curiosity wasn't quick enough. Not as fast as Fergal's.

Got it!

He held it tight, rattled it. The lady had been right. It was light, all but empty, with just a little something — a little, special, mysterious *something* — locked away inside.

"Twenty pence, love."

He paid. As he did, his phone rang.

"Hello, Dad."

"Where are you? You're late."

"Just coming."

Fergal got his change and ran as fast as he could, the length of the concourse, and didn't stop till he got to the entrance of the golf shop.

"I see you bought something."

"Hi, Dad. Just a can, for my collection."

Judging from the bags by his feet, Mr. Bamfield had bought a few things for his golf club collection as well.

"Just one or two golfing items," he mumbled. "No need to say too much to your mother."

"Probably no need to mention my can either, then," Fergal said. His father nodded curtly.

They drove back to the house. Fergal sat holding the bag with his new trousers in it and, on top of that, his can. He felt a warm glow of pride, a sense of achievement, as if, after extensive searching and much digging, he had finally unearthed buried treasure.

As soon as they got home, he would ring Charlotte. He wouldn't open the can until she was there. They would open it together.

This one might contain a vital clue, some small but essential key to unlock the mysteries of the cans.

"Come round here if you like," Charlotte said over the phone. "Can you get a lift?"

"It's not far, I'll walk."

"Will they let you?"

"I think so. Half an hour, then?"

"Okay."

"Right."

Fergal hung up then went to find his father. He'd be the one to ask. His mother would have doubts and worries. His father would probably let him do it.

"Dad?"

He was out in the garden, practicing swings with his new golf club.

"Hmm?"

"Can I walk round to Charlotte's?"

"On your own?"

"I was all right in the mall. It's only ten minutes to get there. Fifteen at the most."

"Oh . . . I suppose so. If you take your phone. I dare say you're old enough. In fact, when I was your age . . ."

Only Fergal didn't have time for the reminiscences just then, interesting as they might be.

"Okay, Dad. Thanks. See you later."

"What are you doing with that can?"

"Taking it with me. Thought I might show it to Charlotte."

"But . . ."

But Fergal had gone. His father swiped at the grass with his golf club. Had he done things like that at Fergal's age? Had weird hobbies? Maybe he had. Yes. Maybe he had, at that. It was just a few cans anyway. Just a few boring old cans from the bargain basket.

What harm could there be in them?

***

"Listen."

Fergal shook it next to her ear.

"Let me."

She reached and shook the can herself.

"You think it's another bit of the body?"

"If it is, it's a small one. Where's the opener?"

"Here. I brought it up earlier, just after you phoned."

"Go on then. You open it. I found it, so you can open it. That's fair."

"Right."

Charlotte first went to the door of her room to make sure that they wouldn't be disturbed. She looked out, closed the door softly, then returned to the can. She took the opener and began to open it.

"Well?"

"Hold on."

She tipped the can's contents out onto her desk.

"Is it a bit of body?"

"No. It's a piece of paper."

Charlotte showed it to Fergal. It was a small piece of paper, folded over upon itself until it could be folded no more. It looked grubby and gray.

"Let's see."

Fergal picked up the pellet of paper and began to unfold it. He flattened it out on the desk and smoothed it with his hand. Then suddenly that hand began to tremble slightly and his face took on a corpse-like pallor.

"There's a m-m . . ." The words wouldn't come out. Fergal swallowed and tried again. "There's a m-message."

Charlotte stared at him, her eyes wide and curiously magnified behind the lenses of her glasses.

"What does it say?"

"Read it."

Charlotte peered down at the grubby piece of paper. Written upon its crumpled and crinkled surface, with what must surely have been a blunt stub of pencil, was one solitary word. The hand that had written it seemed childish, or certainly uneducated, a hand which had not had much experience or practice at writing. The message had been printed, not in capitals, but in lowercase letters. They were not, however, joined up, just written out separately. There were four of them: one vowel and three consonants. They spelled the word *h e l p*.

11. CODE CRACKERS

"We ought to go to the police now," Fergal said.

"They'll never believe us," Charlotte told him. "They'll say we wrote it ourselves. They'll never believe we found it in a can."

"They will when they see we've got an ear and a finger to go with it."

"Umm. Maybe," Charlotte reluctantly agreed.

She could see that perhaps Fergal was right. They should go to the police, and hand everything over to them, the finger, the ear, the ring, the stud, and now the note with the word *help* written on it, and leave the rest to them.

But in all honesty, she didn't want to, and neither did Fergal, if he was equally truthful. It was something you wanted to work out alone and then go to the police afterward, when you had all the evidence and all the answers to give them, and all they had to do was to go and make arrests. You didn't want them to solve the mystery; you wanted to solve it for yourself.

Who did the cans belong to, anyway? Who were the ones who had taken up the hobby in the first place, when nobody else was interested, when everyone thought that it was a pretty stupid pastime, in fact?

That's right. Fergal for one, Charlotte for another; and you didn't discover the most interesting, fascinating cans in the world, just to hand your secrets over to somebody else to fathom. It was for them to get to the bottom of the cans. It was their duty, their responsibility.

"How about," Charlotte suggested, "that we don't go to the police for *now*, but we go to the police *soon*? If we can't solve things ourselves?"

Fergal looked at her quizzically.

"How long's *soon*?" he said, liking to have matters clear in his mind.

Charlotte shrugged. "What about — a couple of days or so?"

"You don't think that's too *soon*?" Fergal said.

"How about — as soon as we can, then?" Charlotte said. "When we feel the time is right? We'll play it by ear — so to speak."

Fergal nodded.

"Okay," he agreed. "And besides, I know, the note says *help*, but it doesn't say *Urgent!*, does it? Maybe they can hang on a while. So if we don't get any leads within a reasonable time, we'll go to the police. Agreed?"

Charlotte nodded. She and Fergal eyed each other with mutual, silent understanding, conspiracy implicit in their glances.

"Good," Fergal said. "That'll give us a chance to get to the bottom of it and then we can really show them."

It was Charlotte's turn to look puzzled.

"Show who? Show them what?"

"The people who go around saying that we're clever, when what they really mean is they think we're stupid."

"Right," Charlotte said. She turned her attention back to the note. "We'd better get on with it. Let's see what we can make of this."

Charlotte picked up the piece of paper and looked at it through her spectacles. It was ragged and torn along one edge, and triangular in shape.

"Looks like somebody ripped it off something."

"A paper bag, maybe."

"Or the corner of an envelope."

"So what can we tell from that, then?" Fergal said.

Charlotte thought awhile.

"Dunno. Got any suggestions?"

"No," Fergal said.

"Okay. Let's think about it logically for five minutes. You come up with an explanation and I'll come up with an explanation, then we'll go on from there."

They sat in silence. Charlotte's clock ticked the seconds away. The seconds turned to minutes and soon the time was up.

"Well?" she said.

Fergal had been staring out of the window. He turned and faced her.

"Okay. How's this? Someone — let's say it's a he — is being held prisoner . . . in some kind of factory . . . where they put things in cans. He knew he was going to be murdered and he had no way of getting help. The only way he could think of was to get a message into a can somehow. So he managed to do that. He knew his hope of the message being found by somebody eventually was quite good — because all cans must get opened in the end. But he also knew that his chances of being saved were still very slim. Because you don't know when someone will open a can. It might sit in the pantry for years. And also, it's one thing to find a can, it's another to discover where it came from. In a way, it's like someone on a desert island putting a message into a bottle . . ."

"A message in a can, in fact," Charlotte interjected.

"Precisely. You put a message into a bottle, you throw it into the ocean, and you let the tide and the currents take it. It might travel for years and never be found. It might travel thousands of miles, it might only travel two or three. But it might save your life in the end."

"But why wouldn't you say in the note where you were, so that people could find you?"

"Because," Fergal said, "you wouldn't necessarily know where you were. This man in the factory, it was like he'd been shipwrecked. Sure, you know you're on an island — but what island? Same for him. He knew he was in a factory — but what factory? Where? Maybe that part he didn't know. Or maybe he didn't have time to write it down. Or maybe he only had this little bit of paper. Or —"

"All right!" Charlotte said, fearing he would never stop. "No need to go on forever. I take your point. And so?"

"Well, that's it," Fergal said. "That's my explanation."

"So what about the finger and the ear and the ring and the stud?"

"Oh yes. That bit. Well, he was too late."

"How d'you mean?"

"With the note. They chopped him up and put him in cans, and by the time the note was discovered, it was all too late and he couldn't be rescued."

"But why would they put him in cans?" Charlotte said. "Like you say, all cans get opened eventually. If you're going to murder somebody, you don't want people finding the evidence. So why put the person in cans? When people find bits of bodies in cans, well, they're bound to go to the police."

Fergal gave her a long, cool look.

"We haven't," he reminded her.

"True," Charlotte had to admit. "But all the same, if I was a murderer and I had a body to get rid of, I'd go and bury it somewhere or throw it into the sea with a paving slab tied to its leg, so that it could never, ever be found. I wouldn't stick it in a can and send it off to the supermarket. No way."

Fergal sighed. He didn't say so, but he had to agree with her. His explanation was all right as far as it went — it just didn't actually go very far.

"Go on, then," he said. "So what's your theory?"

Charlotte sat down on her bed and hugged her knees with her arms.

"Well, it isn't a theory, exactly," she said. "It's more a series of points."

"Go on."

"Well, first of all, how did these cans ever get out of the factory?"

"On a truck, probably."

"No. I don't mean that. I mean, how did they ever get past all the checks and the controls that there must be? Surely, when you're running a factory, you have quality control and supervisors and people making sure that nothing substandard gets out."

"I see what you mean," Fergal conceded. "You mean all the cans are probably automatically weighed, and things like that."

"Yes."

"So how did they get past all the checks then?" he said.

Charlotte took a moment to answer.

"They don't have any checks," she said.

"But why wouldn't they?"

"Because it's a rotten factory. It's old-fashioned, it's substandard, and it's second-rate, and they don't care what goes out as long as they make money."

"How do you work that out?"

"Well, think about it. For a start, the labels keep coming off. I mean, okay, labels get torn off cans all the time. Maybe when they're unpacked in the warehouse they get a bit of rough handling, or maybe someone drops a pallet of cans from the forklift truck as they're unloading the truck, and you end up with a few dozen dented ones and ones with no labels. But the labels are coming off these cans all the time. And why's that? Well, because they're not being put on properly in the first place. Because it's a cheap, nasty factory, they use cheap, nasty glue which doesn't stick very well, and they don't have any quality control to ensure that substandard and underweight cans don't make it off the conveyor belt."

Fergal nodded. He had to agree that it made a certain amount of sense.

"And I'll tell you something else," Charlotte plowed on, "which makes me think it's an old-fashioned and substandard factory: the cans themselves."

"What about them?" Fergal said.

She gave him a look of reproach. What kind of a can collector was he to ask a question like that?

"Look at this one," she said.

Charlotte took the now-empty can and placed it on the bed. Then she took an unopened can without a label from her collection and placed that beside the first one.

"See?"

"See what?"

She shot him another withering glance.

"Look at the metal. It just looks cheap. And this can has to be opened with a can opener. Most of the popular and well-known brands have gone over to ring-pull cans. You don't need an opener for them, you just grab the ring and yank the top off and there you are. So my theory is that whatever they make in this factory, it's some kind of economy brand, something cheap, something they're none too fussy about. Something like . . ."

"Like what?"

"I . . . don't know," Charlotte had to admit.

Fergal looked despondent. He had thought that she was going to come up with the answer right there and then.

"Me neither," he said.

Charlotte brightened up.

"But maybe there's a way to find out."

"How?"

"We keep searching the supermarkets."

"For what?"

"For cans like this one. Cheap-looking cans. Cans whose labels aren't stuck on very well and are peeling away."

"But that wouldn't prove anything. There might be loads of cheap and nasty factories making cheap and nasty canned goods with the labels peeling away."

"But if we find the right cans, the same as this, only with the labels still on, then we'll have the brand name, won't we? And most labels, as well as the manufacturer's name, usually have an address too. Then we'll know where the Help note came from, where it was put into the can." Charlotte's voice dropped to a half-whisper. "And we'll know where the chopped-off finger came from . . . and the severed ear. And even if it's too late for the person who wrote the note, there might still be others in the same predicament."

"Yes, but how can we know — even if we do find the right brand — that it *is* the right brand?"

"From these," Charlotte said.

She upturned the can that had contained the note and pointed to the series of numbers and letters printed on the bottom.

"See? The serial number. I reckon that if we can find cans on the supermarket shelves with the same, or at least very similar, numbers to these, we'll have found the right brand and the right factory."

"Wait," Fergal said."If what you're saying is true, then . . . have you still got the can the ear came in?"

"Yes. Of course."

"And the one with the ring?"

"Yes."

"Let's see them."

Charlotte went to the wardrobe, opened a drawer, rummaged about in it, and produced the two cans. She brought them over to the bed and put them next to the can that had contained the Help note.

"Okay. Turn them over."

Charlotte did so. There, on the bottoms of the cans, were the serial numbers and codes.

"Gimme a pencil."

Fergal passed her a pencil and a piece of paper from her desk.

"Right. Read it out."

"Okay." Fergal picked up the can that had contained the note. There was a seventeen-character code on the base of the can. He read it out and Charlotte wrote each digit down.

"DFBN161."

"Got that."

"4590."

"4590."

"23:35."

"Got that."

"AO."

"Right."

"Okay. I'll read the code out from one of the other cans now. Was this the one that had the ear in it?"

"Yes. I marked it with a Magic Marker. It's got an E written there, see?"

"Okay. Here's the code."

"Ready."

"It's — DFBN148 1190 14:17 AO."

"Okay. And the can that had the ring in it?"

"DFBN120 121280 18:05 AO."

"Right."

"Let's see."

Charlotte placed the paper down upon the duvet so that they could both see the three codes, written one under the other.

DFBN161 4590 23:35 AO.

DFBN148 1190 14:17 AO.

DFBN120 121280 18:05 AO.

"One of the codes is longer than the others," Fergal pointed out. "Why's that?"

"We'll have to work it out. Start at the beginning. The first four letters are always the same."

"They must identify something, then."

"Like what's in the can?"

"Yes. The product, or where it was made . . . what factory it was made in — manufacturer's name perhaps, something like that."

"Then there's three numbers."

"Maybe they're batch numbers."

"Maybe that's what the BN means. Batch number . . ."

"Followed by the number."

"So DF means what?"

"Stands for what's in the can?"

"Maybe. What's next?"

"4590, 1190, and 121280."

"Got to stand for something."

"Maybe they're dates?" Fergal suggested.

"Dates? What kind of dates?"

"Sell-by dates, use-by dates . . . They'd print them on the labels for the customers. Only here, in the manufacturing serial number, they've coded them a little."

"How?"

"Turned them round. Look, say 90 stands for 2009, and 80 for 2008 . . ."

"That would make sense, because the one with 80 on it also has an earlier batch number."

"So 4590 would mean the fourth day of the fifth month of 2009. The fourth of May."

"And 1190 would mean the first of January."

"And 121280 would mean the twelfth of December, 2008."

"What's after that?"

"23:35, 14:17 and 18:05. Must be the time of day."

"Yes. On the twenty-four-hour clock. To tell you what time the can was sealed or something like that."

"So what about AO?" Fergal said. "The last bit?"

"Must be another identifier of some kind. It's the same on all three cans, so it must have something to do with the contents of the can or the place they were made. So that's what we have to look for — DFBN, followed by a batch number, followed by a date, followed by a time, followed by AO."

Fergal squinted at Charlotte.

"When you say, 'that's what we have to look for,' what do you mean, exactly?"

"I mean we have to go through all the cans in the supermarkets we bought these from, looking for a similar code. Once we find it, we're on our way to knowing where the note came from . . . and the ring . . . and the finger."

"Yes, but *all* the cans?" Fergal said. "*All* the cans, Charlotte? In how many supermarkets? Have you any idea how many cans that is? Talk about needles in haystacks! To look at the bottom of every single can in a supermarket — that would take . . . forever. How are we going to do it? We'll get thrown out. We can't go round looking at every single can. They'll think we're loonies."

"Well, to start with, we don't actually have to look at the bottom of *every* can. Just at one of every type of can. You don't have to look at every can of Camberwell's Tomato Soup, for instance — just one, to see what the code looks like. If it's not the code we're after, then forget about it and on to the next. Just looking at one will be enough."

Fergal could see the sense in it. He nodded and said, "Yes. Okay. But even so, it's still going to take a long time. And how are we going to do it?"

"The only way we can," Charlotte said. "One shelf at a time. We'll concentrate on the supermarket we met in first. How often do you go shopping there?"

"About once a week, with my mum."

"Me too. But that'll never do it. We'll have to get over there every chance we get. If anyone asks questions, you can say you're at my house and I'll say I'm round at yours. We'll be helping each other with projects or something."

"And it *is* a sort of project too," Fergal pointed out.

"Yes," Charlotte said. "A *very urgent* sort of project. Okay. So we'll divide that supermarket in half. You do one lot of shelves, I'll do the other. Then we'll visit all the other supermarkets we've got dodgy cans from, and we just keep going until we find the cans with the right code."

"And if we do . . ."

"Not *if*, Fergal — *when*."

"Okay. And *when* we do then?"

"Then we have to investigate, don't we? We have, like they say on *Crime Scene*, to make our inquiries and to pursue our investigations."

"That," Fergal pointed out, "might be dangerous. We're not dealing with a bunch of stamp collectors here, you know. We're dealing with a cut-off finger and a severed ear and a note that says *help*. Finding where these cans have come from could actually be highly dangerous indeed."

"Yes," Charlotte nodded. "It could well be dangerous. Interesting though, isn't it? Or would you rather go to the police now? Only don't forget, they'd be starting from scratch. Whereas we're already on the case. So? Do we carry on?"

But that question required no answer. She knew it and so did Fergal.

The two of them sat a while, contemplating the cans and the ragged note reading *help*.

Fergal tried to calculate how long it would take them to check each type of can in a supermarket. Quite a while, he reckoned. You'd really need somebody like Hercules for a task like that.

"It's a big job, isn't it?" Charlotte said, seeming to echo his thoughts.

"Yes." He nodded. "It is."

"But we can do it, can't we, Ferg? We can do it together. The two of us."

She'd called him Ferg. No one had ever called him Ferg before. It made him feel all warm inside.

12. BEANS, BEANS, BEANS

"What are you doing, Fergal?"

Why was that? Why was it that whenever you were doing something you didn't want your parents to notice, they noticed it? And, similarly, why was it that when you did want them to notice something — to take a hint about some present you wanted, or to realize how desperately in need of chocolate or ice cream or extra pocket money you were — they noticed nothing at all?

"I'm just looking, Mum, at the . . . the cans."

"Canned prunes, Fergal? Since when did you like prunes?"

"Er, no, I don't really . . . I just like . . . sort of . . . looking at them."

Mrs. Bamfield picked up a can of pears and put it into the trolley. In her opinion, this obsession with cans had gone too far. It was time for Fergal to take up another hobby. Collecting the things was bad enough, going round reading them was even worse.

"If you want something to read, Fergal, I'll buy you a book. It really isn't necessary to go around the supermarket reading the bottoms of cans. I mean, you do have a library card, you know."

"Yes, Mum," Fergal said, replacing the canned prunes and picking up some mandarin oranges. He turned the can over and looked at the code. No. That wasn't it either. There was no similarity at all. It was a twelve-digit code and had nothing in common with the one he was looking for.

Fergal put the oranges back on the shelf and took up a can of peaches.

"Fergal!"

"Mum?"

"You're still doing it!"

"What?"

"Reading the bottoms of cans. Whatever are you doing it for?"

"Oh, you know . . . I'm just interested."

"Is this to do with being clever, Fergal?"

"Er . . . could be," he said vaguely.

"Well, I hope it is. I hope it is to do with being clever and not anything to do with the opposite of clever, as I sometimes fear it might."

"Oh no, Mum," Fergal reassured her. "It's definitely to do with being clever."

He was prepared to say anything, just as long as he was left in peace to look at his cans.

At first he and Charlotte had thought they would divide the supermarket up between them and do half each. But Charlotte had pointed out that it would be quite easy for either of them to miss a section. It wouldn't be possible to read all the codes on all the tins in one shopping session. It might take two, three, or even more. The local supermarket was a huge place — more hyper than super. You could have parked a few airplanes in it without any trouble.

It would be quite easy, Charlotte continued, to forget where you had left off and to come back the following day and start a bit farther on from where you had finished. That way you would be bound to miss a crucial section and the cans with the right codes on them might never be found.

"So it is best if we both do it," she said. "It's twice the work, but it's also twice the security. That way there's less likelihood of us missing anything — always assuming there's something there at all."

"And why wouldn't there be?" Fergal asked.

"They might have stopped stocking whatever it is. Or it might be a discontinued line."

"Okay. So we both check everything."

"Right. From start to finish, then. From entrance to exit. From the front door to the till. We both check every brand and type of can there is, and we don't give up until we find the one that matches the code."

"Right."

"Fergal!"

His mother's voice pulled him back sharply to the present.

"Mum?"

"Come along now. We're moving on to the frozen section."

"Right with you. I'll catch up with you."

"Well, see you do. I don't want to have to come back looking for you. I don't have the time. I really don't see what pleasure you get from reading the bottoms of those cans at all, Fergal. They can't tell much of a story, I wouldn't have thought."

Fergal watched as she moved on, taking the trolley with her. He wished he could explain it to her, but she'd never really understand, never believe him either . . . unless he showed her the finger.

Fergal replaced the peaches and took up a can of strawberries. He looked at the code. No. That wasn't it either.

He moved on down the aisle. He had to be methodical and systematic about this. No doing a can here and a can there, no flitting from shelf to shelf like a bee in a garden, buzzing from flower to flower. He had to start at the beginning and go all the way to the end, can by can, display by display, aisle by aisle.

It took him ages just to do all the canned fruits. There were so many of them. There were canned blackberries, canned gooseberries, canned apples, canned mangoes — you name it. Then next to the fruit were canned pie filling and canned rice pudding, then canned custards and canned creamy desserts, which also seemed to go on forever.

Fergal kept an eye on the clock as he proceeded down along the aisle. His mother would take about twenty minutes to finish her shopping. As long as he was standing near the checkout section by then, to meet her and help pack, there wouldn't be any trouble.

Finally he finished the aisle. He looked back along the length of it, just to ensure that he hadn't missed anything. No. He had done them all. He had checked at least one can of each variety and none of them had matched the codes, which he had written down on a scrap of paper in his pocket, but which by now were also committed to memory.

Right. He turned the corner and walked into the next aisle.

His heart sank.

Cans.

There were miles of them. Miles and miles of cans. They seemed to go on to infinity.

It was the aisle with the baked beans, the sweet corn, the soup, the pasta, the spaghetti, and canned vegetables and convenience meals. There seemed to be about fifty different varieties of beans alone. There were kidney beans, green beans, adzuki beans, butter beans, French beans. There were baked beans with sausage and baked beans with bacon. There were low-calorie baked beans, low-sodium baked beans, organic baked beans, environmentally friendly baked beans, and beans labeled "suitable for vegetarians." There were the supermarket's own label baked beans standing alongside the more famous ones. There were economy baked beans. There were individual-portion-size servings of baked beans. There were ordinary-size servings of baked beans. There were family-size cans of baked beans. There were big-family-size cans of baked beans. There were very-big-family-size cans of baked beans. There were barbecue-flavored baked beans. There were beans in tomato sauce. There were spicy baked beans and curried baked beans, beans with additives and beans without. There were beans and beans and beans.

And that was just the beans. The baked ones.

And next to the shelves of baked beans were the canned spaghet-tis and pastas. All sorts of them. SpaghettiOs, spaghetti bolognese, pasta shapes, alphabet pasta . . .

Suddenly it struck Fergal, more forcibly than ever, the full enormity, the immensity of the task that he and Charlotte had taken on. But then he felt too that they were equal to it. The cans, the strange objects inside them, the note itself . . . surely these things hadn't come to them by accident alone? It was more than chance, it was destiny — as if he and Charlotte had been personally chosen to solve the mystery by some higher power.

Only it might already be too late.

As Fergal contemplated all the tins in the length of the supermarket aisle, as he saw them recede into the distance, he realized that this was an ocean too. It may not be marked on any map or in any atlas. But this also was a great, huge, uncharted sea. And every day of his life, waves of cans surged along, they traveled up the motorways and into supermarkets. There were oceans of beans, torrents of spaghetti, tidal waves of tomato soup.

Everywhere you looked, there were cans. People came and bought them and took them home, they opened them up, devoured their contents, and then . . .

Where did they all go? All the empty cans? Some were recycled, maybe, but the rest just went to the rubbish tip. The oceans then turned into mountains, into peaks the size of Everest, into huge, towering skyscrapers, made entirely out of . . . cans.

Fergal felt that he was going under, drowning in deep fathoms of cans. He had visions of mermaids, their tails fashioned from recycled tin cans, their fins made out of old ring-pulls. He saw Neptune, only instead of clutching a trident in his hand, he was grasping a great big can opener.

It was hopeless — futile. He was never going to find the right can. They were never going to find it. It was impossible. He wanted to give up. He wanted a lifeboat to come and rescue him, to carry him to dry, can-free land.

But then he remembered the scrap of paper. It could have been written by someone just like him, a child. It must have been written by somebody who had nobody, who had nothing, not even hope. Somebody with no one to turn to. Somebody desperate and in terrible trouble. Someone in danger, someone in fear. Only who and what and where? And why?

Fergal realized that he couldn't give up. Because there was only him. He and Charlotte were the ones Fate had picked out to shoulder this burden. So even if he had to wade through a million cans of beans, he couldn't give up until he had done so.

He could leave no stone — and no can — unturned.

Begin at the beginning, then. Where else was there to start? Begin at the beginning, end at the end. There was no other way to do it. He reached out for the first can of beans. And the next. And the next after that. Until . . .

"Fergal! There you are! I thought I told you not to go wandering and to meet me at the checkout. I did say that I didn't want to have to come looking for you — did I not?"

"Er, yes, Mum."

"What did I say?"

"That you didn't want to come looking for me and I should meet you by the checkout."

"Exactly. And what have I had to do, Fergal?"

"Come looking for me, Mum."

"Yes, Fergal. And where are you?"

"Er . . . not by the checkout."

"Precisely. And you're going to make us late. So come along. Let's get to the checkout and get on home."

"Okay, Mum. I'll just read the bottom of this . . ."

But Mrs. Bamfield had finally arrived at the end of her tether. She snatched the can of beans from Fergal and replaced it on the shelf.

"*Now*, Fergal!" she said. "Not later, not this afternoon, not tomorrow, not next week. Now. We go now!"

So Fergal had to leave the unchecked cans behind him and follow his mother to the till. He was another day away from solving the mystery, another day away from helping whoever had written the note.

And what did that mean for them?

He wished he could tell his mother about it. He really did. But he knew that she would never believe him.

When they got home he telephoned Charlotte.

"Any luck?" he asked her.

"Not been yet," she said. "We're going this afternoon. You?"

"No. I've done canned fruit and puddings and was just starting on the beans, but I had to go. There are an awful lot of cans to get through, you know. An awful lot."

"Well, I'm afraid you're going to have to do most of them on your own," Charlotte said, "after today."

Fergal swallowed, shocked and surprised. What on earth did she mean? Was she leaving it all up to him?

"What . . . ?"

"It's half-term next week," Charlotte said, "and we're off on holiday. We're taking an extra week, on top of the usual. I'm sorry. It's not that I don't want to help, I just can't."

"But . . . but what about whoever wrote the note? Another few weeks, I mean, by the time we get to them, they might be . . . well . . . dead."

"I know," Charlotte said. "But what can I do? I can't announce to my parents that I'm not going on holiday with them as I wish to spend two weeks in the supermarket looking at the codes on the bottoms of cans — can I? They sprang this trip on me a bit suddenly. It's not that I *want* to go!"

"No," Fergal had to agree, "I suppose not."

"So you'll have to carry on without me. But I'll be back on the case the moment we get home."

"Which will be when, exactly?"

"Three weeks from today."

"Okay. But you're going to the supermarket this afternoon?"

"Sure. And if I find anything, I'll let you know straightaway."

"Okay, Charlotte. But remember, won't you, somebody out there needs our help. We're the only hope they've got."

"I haven't forgotten," Charlotte said. "I'll be in touch."

"OK. Have a good hol —"

But she had already hung up. And she didn't ring back later. So Fergal knew that, like him, she had not had any success in finding matching cans in the supermarket that day.

Nor did Fergal have any success on the following Saturday. He made considerable headway into the cans of beans, of pasta, of peas, of mushrooms, of sweet corn, of everything else in the aisle of canned vegetables and convenience foods, but he did not find what he was looking for.

The weekend after that, however, when Charlotte was halfway through her holiday with her parents, something interesting happened. Something interesting, and something rather peculiar.

Fergal Bamfield went missing.

Fergal Bamfield completely vanished.

PART 3

Diary of F. Bamfield.

Month of Whatever.

Not just private but confidential.

No interfering busybodies to read this.

If you are reading this and you are not F. Bamfield, then you are an interfering busybody.

But, hey! I suppose if I found somebody else's diary, I'd read it too.

I don't know when I'll be writing this diary again, if ever, as I am setting off on an expedition.

I've had to take drastic measures. Trouble is, I can't tell anyone, as not only is it hush-hush, it is also very urgent, possibly even dangerous. I could tell Charlotte, but she's not here and no one else would listen.

I suppose the truth is that all my life I've never been brave or done anything that people thought was good or special. But I'm going off to be brave now.

It's a bit scary, but sometimes you have no choice, as people might be depending on you, and you are the only hope they have.

So here I go, then. For better or worse. I hope I get back to write another entry in this diary someday.

If this is Mum or Dad reading this — I love you both.

Please look after Angus and stroke him till he purrs.

13. CANS, CANS, CANS

Cans, cans, cans.

All he could see were cans.

They passed Fergal by regularly, rhythmically.

Cans, cans, cans.

It was like a dream. Lines of cans. They marched past like soldiers off to fight, gleaming and polished, bright in their armor, heading for battle, heading for war. Off they went, toward the transport that would take them to where they had to go, to the front line.

Cans, cans, nothing but cans. No bottles, no glasses, no plastic containers, no lidded jars. Just cans. As they moved along, they rattled and clanged, until finally they came to a halt. That was when Fergal had to play his part, to do his bit, in this world of cans. They were his masters. They had taken him over, and if he didn't do what he had to they would soon be upon him, swarming all over him — the great tyranny of cans.

His limbs ached, but still the cans came. His eyes grew tired, his ears throbbed with the sound, but still they came. He slept, he woke, and there they were, there they always were, the unending procession of cans.

It was like in the cartoon film *Fantasia*, the "Sorcerer's Apprentice" sequence, where the hapless apprentice commanded the broom to do the work, to bring in the buckets of water. But once it started, he hadn't been able to stop it, and the broom turned to other brooms, all carrying even more buckets of water, and still the brooms and the water and the buckets kept coming.

Just like the cans, cans, cans — a great flood of cans.

Fergal's head throbbed. His eyes were rimmed red with tiredness. But still they came. The cans rolled on. Button bright, all standing to attention, trim and disciplined and marching in unison, all in rows, all the same distance apart. On they went, the great legions, the battalions, the foot soldiers, like ants, like lemmings, like a blizzard of snowflakes, like a swarm of locusts — a plague of cans.

You disposed of one, but another was right behind it, or right beside it. There was nothing you could do. You could fight them, but you could never defeat them, this massive army of cans.

Cans.

Cans.

Sometimes Fergal really couldn't stand it anymore, and he let out a long shout of anger and despair.

For a split of a split second they seemed to fall silent. But then the noise of the march resumed. On they came, clanking and clattering, metal and mechanical, unfeeling and uncaring. Mindless. Moronic. Stupid. Relentless.

Unending.

Cans.

***

"Hello, Mrs. Bamfield."

It took a moment before Charlotte realized that something was wrong. She could have telephoned first, but she felt that it would be better to go round in person. After all, she'd even brought a present — a can, as a matter of fact. A foreign can. With an interesting label.

"Is Fergal in?"

Charlotte had a lot to ask him too. If he'd had any luck while she had been away. Whether he had matched the codes up and, if not, how many of the supermarket aisles remained unchecked. She'd sent texts and e-mails while on holiday, asking for a progress report, but Fergal must have been too busy to reply.

"Fergal?"

Mrs. Bamfield looked ghastly, pale, ill. She seemed to have aged years in a matter of weeks. She looked as if she had been dealt some terrible blow. Perhaps some close friend or even a family member had died.

"Yes, Fergal. Is he in at the moment?"

It crossed Charlotte's mind that Mrs. Bamfield didn't actually recognize her. She was staring at her as though she simply didn't know who she was.

"I've got a present for him," Charlotte explained. "I brought it back from holiday — in France. Mrs. Bamfield . . . are you all right?"

Charlotte realized now that Fergal's mother's eyes were red, puffy, and swollen. She had been crying. And by the look of the dark rings underneath her bloodshot eyes, she hadn't been sleeping much either.

"Mrs. Bamfield . . . ?"

Fergal's mother stood there in the doorway of the house, neither inviting Charlotte in nor asking her to go. An awful, uncomfortable silence grew, like some great festering weed.

"Mrs. Bamfield . . . are you okay?"

Then she seemed to see her at last, to know who she was.

"Charlotte . . ."

"Yes, Mrs. Bamfield. It's me, Charlotte. The can collector. Fergal's friend, remember? We met in the supermarket when we were reaching for the same can in the bargain basket. You do remember me, don't you, Mrs. Bamfield? You just don't look very well."

Mrs. Bamfield's hand went to her sleeve. She pulled out a handkerchief and pressed it to one of her eyes.

"Oh, Charlotte, Charlotte . . ." she began. "Of course, you've been away, haven't you? You wouldn't know, would you? You wouldn't know. And you're his only friend, really. I mean, he's got other friends, but you seemed to understand, didn't you, my dear? A proper, true friend. . . . Do come in for a moment, please."

Charlotte nodded and followed her into the house. They sat in the quiet kitchen. The fridge murmured, the clock ticked. The place seemed unnaturally tidy. Mrs. Bamfield was too preoccupied with whatever it was that had so upset her even to offer Charlotte so much as a glass of water, let alone some orange juice or a cookie, as she would normally have done.

"What's happened, Mrs. Bamfield? It's Fergal, isn't it?"

"Yes, it is. It is. He's gone."

Charlotte looked at her. She didn't immediately understand.

"Gone? You mean . . . gone out? He'll be back later?"

"No, no," Mrs. Bamfield said. "We don't know if he'll ever be back at all."

"But gone . . . gone where?"

"If only we knew," Mrs. Bamfield said. "But we've no idea. We've searched everywhere, the police, everyone, they've all searched everywhere, they're still searching now. Oh, they've been so kind, dear. Everyone's been so very kind. But they haven't found him. Not anywhere. Nor any trace of him either. Nothing at all."

"But what happened? I mean, how . . . where . . . when did he go missing?"

"Last Saturday."

"Last Saturday?"

"Yes. We went to the supermarket, same as usual, in the morning, only this time . . ."

"Yes?"

"Well, this time, instead of my having to drag Fergal out of the place . . . he'd developed this new obsession, you see . . . well, hobby, he'd have called it . . . it's because he's so clever, you know . . . at least . . . because he was so clever . . ." Her hands began to tremble. "What if I never see him again . . . ?"

"Oh, Mrs. Bamfield, you mustn't talk like that."

"I know, dear, I know I shouldn't. But it's been so long now, a whole week, that I've started to think the worst. What if he's been abducted? Or had a terrible accident? If he's lying unconscious somewhere, or alone and afraid, or . . ."

Charlotte stared at her, full of questions, yet not knowing what to say. Seeing that Mrs. Bamfield wasn't capable of offering her a glass of water, Charlotte fetched one for Mrs. Bamfield instead. She wondered where Mr. Bamfield was.

"He's out looking for him," Mrs. Bamfield explained, seeming to guess her thoughts. "He's out looking for Fergal every minute of the day. He says he'll find him. He says he won't stop until he does . . . but what if he doesn't? What if we never see Fergal again? If only he'd come back, if only he would. It wouldn't matter about him being a bit clumsy and awkward and having funny hobbies. He could have all the strange hobbies he wanted to. Not just fifty cans, but a hundred, a thousand. He could fill the whole house with cans, and with sacks of rubbish if he wanted to, or cardboard boxes, or moldy old newspapers, if only he'd come back."

Mrs. Bamfield went to the sink and took a sponge cloth. She began to wipe down the perfectly clean kitchen counters as if her life and sanity depended on it.

"We had our ups and downs and our little arguments, the way all families do," she went on. "But we got on so well, mostly. He'd never have run away deliberately, I know he wouldn't. And I don't think he was unhappy at school or being bullied or anything like that. If anything, he seemed happier recently, having found a friend like you, Charlotte, to share his interests."

Charlotte felt out of her depth. Dealing with a woman whose son had gone missing wasn't a job for a child her age.

"Is there no one with you, Mrs. Bamfield? To look after you?"

"Oh yes, dear, my sister's here. She's just popped out to the pharmacy for me. She'll be back in a moment."

"Go on, with what you were telling me . . . about Fergal."

Mrs. Bamfield stood wringing the sponge cloth in her hands. Then she resumed her narrative.

"It was last Saturday, as I said. Fergal had got to be very difficult about leaving the supermarket. He'd become obsessed with looking at all the cans — with turning them over and looking at the bottoms of them and checking whatever was on there . . . codes or something, I suppose. Have you any idea why he'd want to do that, Charlotte?"

Charlotte did, but she didn't want to say, at least not until she had heard Mrs. Bamfield's story in full, so she just mumbled, "Maybe," and let Mrs. Bamfield continue.

"But not only had he taken up collecting can numbers — or whatever he was doing — he also had to do it in a methodical way. He had to do all the cans, one aisle at a time, and he seemed to have to check one of every brand and of each variety. If he thought he'd missed one, he'd go back and start again. It was most infuriating, to be honest. I'd be there with a heaped-up trolley, waiting for him at the checkout, only he wouldn't appear and I'd have to go searching for him all over the crowded supermarket. By the time I found him, the lines at the checkouts would be enormous and . . . well, it was most frustrating, anyway, I can tell you that."

"So last week . . ." Charlotte said, trying tactfully to bring Mrs. Bamfield back to the point.

"Yes, anyway, last week it was all different."

"Different? In what way?"

"Last week, he couldn't wait to leave."

"Oh? Really?"

"Yes. It was all very strange. We'd only been there a few minutes . . . well, ten or fifteen anyway . . . and I was pushing the trolley along by the cheese counter, wondering if we should have some Stilton or whether we ought to stick to the Edam, which maybe isn't quite so rich. Mr. Bamfield is very fond of the Stilton himself, and I'm sure it's all right in moderation, but it can't be good for the heart, not in the quantities he eats it, as it's so high in fat and —"

"So you were by the cheese, Mrs. Bamfield?"

"Sorry?"

Charlotte's patience was at breaking point.

"Cheese. You were saying, about Fergal. You were by the cheese when suddenly . . . you were about to tell me something about Fergal?"

"Was I? Oh yes, yes, I was."

Charlotte looked up at the kitchen clock. She wondered how long it might be before Mrs. Bamfield's sister got back.

Mrs. Bamfield forgot the cheese diversion and got back to the point.

"Yes, I was by the cheese counter. To be honest, I'd hardly even begun to do my shopping — because I like to take my time to choose and to sort of plan out a menu for each day of the week, you see — so I'd barely started, as I say, and only had half a dozen items in the trolley, when Fergal suddenly appeared around the aisle, traveling at about a hundred and fifty miles an hour and looking very excited about something."

"Excited? Did he say why? About what?"

Mrs. Bamfield sighed sadly.

"No, dear, he didn't. But he was excited. He had that look in his eye. The Bargain Hunter's Look, I call it. It's that look people get when they've been keeping an eye out for something special for a long time, and suddenly they've found it. I get that feeling myself sometimes, during the January sales."

The code, Charlotte thought. *He must have found the code. He must have found the code on a labeled can. He must have discovered where the strange cans were coming from. And there the manufacturer's name would be, on the label of the can he had found — a name and probably an address too. That must have been it. That must have been why he was so excited. He had matched the code.*

"Did he say what he was excited about, Mrs. Bamfield?"

"No. He didn't. In fact, he wouldn't even admit that he was excited. But he was suddenly in a desperate hurry to get out of the supermarket — quite unlike his usual self, when I practically had to drag him out kicking and screaming. But no. This time he couldn't get me out of the place fast enough. He followed me round every inch of the way, nagging all the time, saying, 'Come on, Mum,' and, 'Mum, do get a move on,' and throwing any old thing into the trolley, just to get me to the till."

"I see."

"And when we got to the pizza, instead of having our usual debates, like we used to do in the old days, when I'd say, 'Which one shall we have, Fergal? Shall we have the margherita or shall we have the pepperoni?' and he'd say, 'Can't we have the four cheeses for a change?' and I'd say, 'We had that two weeks ago. How about having the spinach?' and he'd say, 'I don't like spinach, what about the mushroom?' and I'd say, 'I thought you didn't like mushroom either,' and he'd say . . ."

Charlotte listened with increasing amazement as Mrs. Bamfield prattled on about pizzas. Her distress at Fergal's disappearance seemed to have made her garrulous and unhinged. It was as though if she went on talking about pizzas and cheese counters she wouldn't have to think about Fergal, where he might be, and what had happened to him.

"So he was in a hurry to leave the supermarket?"

Mrs. Bamfield looked at Charlotte as though she had forgotten she was there.

"In a hurry . . . ? Oh yes, yes. He just wanted to go."

"Where did he want to go?"

"Well, just go . . ."

"I see. And I don't suppose you'd know which aisle he came from, Mrs. Bamfield?"

"Aisle?"

"When he arrived all excited and anxious to leave . . . which aisle had he been in?"

Mrs. Bamfield shook her head.

"I wouldn't know, dear. I wouldn't know. Why? Would it matter?"

It was Charlotte's turn to shake her head.

"Probably not," she said. "Not really. So what happened then?"

"Well, I had to put my foot down and insist that we took our time and did our shopping properly. Because you can't hurry good cooking and you can't hurry good shopping either. If you do, you just end up going home with a load of things you didn't want and none of the things you really needed."

"But finally you left."

"Yes. Finally we did. We loaded up the car and drove home. But even as we drove along, Fergal kept saying things like 'Put your foot down, Mum!' and 'Go faster!' and 'There's a gap there' and 'No need to stop, the light's not quite red yet' — which was very unlike him too."

"And then?"

"Well, then we got home. He helped me to carry the shopping in and to unpack it. He seemed to have calmed down a bit by then, or maybe he was only pretending that he had, in order to get round me."

"Get round you?"

"Yes. Because as soon as we'd put the shopping away, he asked me if he could go out."

"Go out?"

"Yes. On his own."

"His own?"

"Yes."

"Where did he want to go to?"

"That was what I asked him."

"And what did he say?"

"'Just out.'"

"Just out?"

"Yes."

"What did you say?"

"'No,' of course. I said that simply wasn't good enough. If he wanted to go out, he would have to tell me exactly where he was going, and even then . . ."

"You weren't very happy about it?"

"No, Charlotte, I was not. And I don't suppose your mother would have been either. I mean, she's obviously let you walk here on your own, but only because it isn't far away and it's broad daylight and it's a respectable neighborhood — though trouble can happen anywhere and bad things can happen to good people, and that's the truth. But she's only let you do it because she feels it's safe. She's probably worrying about you right now and if you're here much longer I wouldn't be surprised to hear the phone ring, and it'll probably be her, asking how you are."

Charlotte nodded.

"Yes," she said. "She insisted I take my mobile so that she could get in touch."

"Exactly, Charlotte," Mrs. Bamfield said. Then her eyes clouded over. "The thing is, you and Fergal, you're getting older and growing up and you need your freedom and your independence. You have to be allowed out on your own sooner or later. Nobody can be kept in and treated like a baby forever. It's just a matter of striking a balance, that's all."

"So you let Fergal go?"

"Yes. Well, first he had to tell me where he was going."

"Where was he going . . . where did he say he was going?"

"To the library and then to the square. He said that some of his schoolmates would be there. They congregate there with their skateboards on a Saturday afternoon and practice their maneuvers or whatever they call them and frighten people — especially ones with strollers — as they zoom by. Fergal doesn't have a skateboard, just Rollerblades, and he didn't even take those, as he's not very good on them, but he said he would go down and watch. I even checked with his father, to see what he thought. He doesn't like me ringing him on the golf course as he's often in the middle of a complicated shot, and if his mobile goes off, he might get distracted and miss it. He won't turn it off though, in case the message is important. So I rang him, and he felt that Fergal would be all right, and so did I. So I let him go."

Mrs. Bamfield paused and reached for her handkerchief.

"I let him go. . . . Why did I let him go, Charlotte? Why did I let him go? If I hadn't, he'd still be here. He'd be here now. He'd still be with us and things would be as they've always been. Fergal with his cans and his other hobbies and life going on and his dad playing golf or going to watch soccer. And all the things I thought were important, all the things I thought mattered, manners and tidiness and all the rest . . . you know, they don't matter at all, Charlotte, not really. People are all that matter. And I wouldn't care if Fergal ate with his elbows on the table forever and ever . . . if only I could have him back."

A great sob racked Mrs. Bamfield and she buried her face in her arms. Charlotte went and fetched her a paper towel. She took it and dried her eyes with it and blew her nose.

"Mrs. Bamfield," Charlotte began to say, "look, the thing is, I realize this might sound crazy, but you know those cans of Fergal's? Well —"

But just then there was the sound of the front door opening and a voice calling, "Only me!"

A woman entered the kitchen. It had to be Mrs. Bamfield's sister, and she carried a small pharmacy bag in her hand.

Charlotte decided that it was time for her to go. She stood up as Fergal's aunt came in.

"Oh. Hello. You've got a visitor?"

"This is a friend of Fergal's, Veronica. Charlotte. She's been away on holiday. She didn't know . . . that he had . . . disappeared."

"Ah. I see. Hello, Charlotte."

"Hello. Actually, I probably ought to be going . . ."

"Okay. Thanks for coming anyway. I'll look after her now."

Charlotte said good-bye to Mrs. Bamfield and said that she hoped Fergal would be found very soon, and she headed for the door.

She closed it quietly behind her and walked down the path. When she got to the gate, she heard the ring tone of a mobile phone.

It was her own. It was her mother, calling to see if she was all right and to ask her where she was.

It was nice to have someone to worry about you. Irritating and annoying, some of the time. But nice too.

***

Charlotte walked home briskly, without even thinking of where she was going. She had to tell somebody now, a grown-up, an adult. She had to tell them all about everything — the cans, the finger, the ring, the severed ear, the gold stud, the note. As soon as she got home she'd tell someone. She'd tell her dad. Or maybe her mum. Or both of them together. Or maybe go to the police. But she had to tell someone. She was out of her depth now. It was all way, way over her head; it was deep, deep water. Deep enough to drown in.

Fergal had found a matching code. He must have. He had discovered the name and the whereabouts of the factory, the place where all the strange cans had come from. And he had foolishly gone off to find it, all on his own, without telling anyone where he was going. He had gone off to the rescue, believing that it couldn't possibly wait a second longer.

And now . . .

Now what?

Well, there was but one possibility, wasn't there?

Whatever had happened to the person who had written that note asking for help . . . whatever terrible thing had happened to them . . . had happened to Fergal too.

Now he needed help as well. And she was the only one who could help him.

But who would believe her?

She could just imagine her own mother's voice, full of disapproval and incredulity.

"Cans, Charlotte! Really! What an idea! Really. How could you? There poor Mr. and Mrs. Bamfield are, absolutely distraught at having lost their son, Fergal, and all you can do to help is to come out with preposterous stories about cans. Honestly, Charlotte, it really isn't good enough. Now go to your room and stay there and think about what you've said, and don't come down until you're ready to say you're sorry and to apologize for telling lies. There's a time and a place for an imagination, and this isn't it. It really isn't appropriate, Charlotte. I thought that we'd brought you up better than this, and we even bought you that new mobile phone as well. And this is how you repay us. By carrying on like this!"

Her ears were ringing with reproaches before she had even spoken a word. No. The truth wouldn't be enough, not without evidence.

But then her heart skipped. She felt lighter, suddenly happier.

She *had* the evidence! Of course! As soon as they saw it they'd believe her. Maybe her story on its own wouldn't convince them, but the severed finger and the cut-off ear would. They were at home, lying in the bottom of the freezer, hidden under all the other things, well wrapped up so no one could see what was inside without undoing all the wrapping.

She hurried on home. As soon as she got in she headed for the utility room, where the freezer was. She went straight to it and opened the door to get the evidence.

Only . . .

The freezer was empty.

Totally empty. There was absolutely nothing in there.

Every single thing had gone.

14. GONE

"Charlotte . . . ?"

"Mum?"

"What are you looking for?"

"I . . . I . . . the . . . the freezer . . ."

"Were you looking for ice cream? Now I told you about helping yourself to ice cream."

"No, no. I wasn't going to take any ice cream. I —"

"Anyway, there isn't any ice cream, if that's what you were looking for."

"But —"

"Or any fudgecicles or any of those lollies you made or anything. All gone, I'm afraid."

"But, Mum . . ."

"Melted."

"Melted?"

"Yes. It must have happened when we were away. Must have been a power cut or something. Anyway, it flipped the trip switch and the freezer must have been off for days. I opened it up to get something out of it, and well . . ."

"Well, what?"

"Disgusting is hardly adequate, Charlotte. Now, excuse me, I want to give it another wipe round, just to be sure. I suppose I ought to leave the door open too, to let the air in."

"You mean everything in the freezer melted?"

"Isn't that what I just said?"

"Everything!"

"Yes. A right horrible mess it was too, Charlotte. Just imagine it. Thawed-out fish, melted ice cream, soggy pizzas, mushy mince, sodden fish fingers, things I'd made and put in there, fruit pies, sauces, gravies, stocks . . . oh, you can't imagine the mess. And the smell when I opened the freezer door. Oh! It smelled as if something had died in there."

"Died?"

"Died. We were lucky the place wasn't full of maggots and bluebottles."

"But, Mum — Mum, that's terrible, that's awful . . ."

"Yes, I know, dear, but it's not so bad; it's all covered under the household insurance. We can go to the supermarket later and stock up with everything. At least it'll all be paid for. It's the mess and the inconvenience more than anything."

"But, Mum — Mum, what did you do with it all?"

Charlotte's mother looked up from her sponge and her cleaning spray and her wiping.

"Do with it, dear?"

"Yes, all the melted things, all the mess."

Charlotte's mother gave a little chuckle.

"I didn't do anything with it, dear." She winked. "I got your father to do all that. I soon got him cracking on the case, with a pair of rubber gloves and a couple of bin liners. He just scooped everything out of there, all into the bin liners, and then off up to the tip."

"The tip! The tip! You threw everything away? You didn't keep anything?!"

Charlotte's mother paused in her wiping.

"Keep anything? You can't be serious, dear. Why would we want to keep anything? Have you ever actually seen a soggy fish finger lying in a pool of melted strawberry ice cream? It isn't what you'd call appetizing, dear, I can tell you that."

"Yes . . . there . . . there was something in there . . ."

"What?"

"There was . . . there was . . ."

Charlotte's mother was looking at her expectantly, but she knew that she couldn't say the words. It was pointless. She would never be believed. Not now, not with the evidence gone.

"There was what, dear?"

"Oh . . . nothing . . . I thought I . . . thought I might have left something in there."

"What?"

"I . . . don't remember."

"Really, Charlotte, whatever are you on about? Now come on, excuse me, out of the way. I must get this cleaned out thoroughly before I turn it back on and get it to its operating temperature."

"Okay."

Charlotte headed for the door.

"Mum . . . ?"

"Umm?"

"Where did Dad take everything?"

"I told you, dear. To the tip. You don't want soggy food hanging around, all going moldy and the flies getting at it, do you?"

"No, Mum, I suppose not."

"So how's Fergal, by the way? You didn't stay there long. You haven't fallen out, have you?"

Charlotte wished she didn't have to tell her mother what had happened. She wished that somebody else could do it. But there was no one else. Only her.

". . . Fergal's disappeared."

Her mother looked up from the freezer.

"He's done *what*?"

***

Cans. They were all right in moderation. But then, wasn't everything? Cans. The sight, the noise, the repetitious movement, the monotony, the endlessness of cans.

Fergal picked up another batch and began to pack them in the box. The instant he did, the conveyor brought more. Each box held one hundred and forty-four cans, they were packed in twelves, twelve along, twelve across. Would this be it forever now, he wondered? Nothing but cans? Or was there an escape from them? Could he escape? The others hadn't managed, had they? They had tried and failed, and their very attempt was, in fact, responsible for bringing him there. The futile attempts of others to escape the trap had lured him into it. And if he tried to escape now himself, or to put his own message into a bottle, his own plea for help, and if he threw it out into the vast ocean of the world, would somebody come to his rescue? And succeed in rescuing him and the others? Or would they too be ensnared forever, like rats in a trap?

He thought of Charlotte, of how they had once agreed that they would go to the police "soon." He hoped she would realize that "soon" had finally come.

He dropped the cans into the box, closed the lid, and pushed it on its way. It rattled off down a set of metal rollers, to where someone else was waiting. The person there tore a length of tape from a dispenser and used it to seal the lid of the box. Then on it went, down the rollers, toward the dispatch bay.

More cans were coming.

"Where's the box?!"

It wasn't ready. The boxes came in flat packs and had to be made up. Xavier, the box maker, had fallen asleep. Fergal turned and saw him, there he was, standing upright, head against a pillar, a flat piece of cardboard in his arms, fast, fast asleep — so fast he was at a standstill.

"The box! Quick! The box!"

Fergal shook him awake. The box maker looked around, bleary-eyed, not knowing where he was, expecting to see green fields and a blue horizon or perhaps an azure sea. But not this. Anything, anywhere but this. Not this drab dullness, this flaking paint and clanking machinery and the eternal procession of silver soldiers, with their label uniforms and shiny helmets.

Run, run, the cans are coming.

"The cans!" Fergal shouted. "The cans! Where's the box? The cans!"

If the box maker didn't do his job, Fergal couldn't do his. There was no time for friendship, pleasantries, no chance to pass the time of day, to chat or to share memories and personal details and reminiscences of a former life. Everything was subservient to the cans.

The box maker stared at him, goggle-eyed, bewildered by tiredness. What was he doing here? And what was he supposed to do?

"The box! The box!" Fergal shouted angrily. "I need a box!"

He was grabbing cans off the conveyor now and stacking them on the floor. There was nowhere else to put them, nowhere else for them to go. If he didn't stack them, they would just roll off the end of the conveyor belt and bang and clatter on to the floor. They would fall, like drops from a tap, splish-splosh into a sink. But when they landed they might get damaged, be dented and bashed, and sooner or later D.S. would come to check up on him, come to see that he was working fast enough. And when he saw the damaged cans, lying on the cold concrete floor, there would be trouble, big, big trouble.

The sort of trouble you didn't want to get into. The kind it was hard to get out of.

"Quick! Quick!"

The box maker struggled to assemble the flat box. The sides and the bottom slotted together. It was easy enough to do, even if the repetition made it dull and deadly boring. Doing it all day or half the night made your arms sore and your shoulders ache. Yes, it was easy enough once you had got into a rhythm and a routine. But break that for a moment, lose momentum, lose the beat, and suddenly you were fingers and thumbs, clumsy and useless, not able to piece things together anymore.

"Come on, come on, come on!" Fergal hissed. "Come on!"

But the box maker couldn't do it. His hands were tired and useless. He couldn't do it anymore. He started to cry.

And still the cans kept coming. Fergal grabbed another wave of them and stacked them on the floor.

"We're falling behind. We'll never catch up if we let it go on. Quick!"

But it was no use. The box maker was sitting crying now, fumbling with the flat cardboard, looking like someone trying to make a complicated piece of origami.

Fergal's anger turned to pity. He grabbed the box maker by the scruff of his shirt and pulled him to his feet.

"Take over the cans! Stack them. On the floor. And don't drop any."

Mechanically, moving like a robot, the box maker obeyed. He seemed able to manage this. Reach, pick up, put down. Reach, pick up, put down.

Towers of cans began to take shape on the floor; first one, then another. Fergal made the box up. Then he took another piece of cardboard. The can towers grew higher. Reach, pick up, put down. Higher still. Fergal reached for another piece of flat cardboard, began to make up another box. Still the cans kept coming. The towers became a city now; the city went on growing.

"Okay. Both of us!" yelled Fergal.

Three boxes made. Three boxes backlog, three boxes behind. Still the cans kept coming.

"Into the boxes. The cans on the floor. And the ones on the conveyor belt too. Don't let them fall."

Fergal and Xavier worked swiftly and smoothly now.

The crisis was abating. The box maker seemed able to cope again.

"That's one of them."

Fergal hoisted the heavy box full of cans up from the floor and set it on the rollers. Away it went to the lid sealer, with his band of tape, then on to the dispatch bay, rolling through a hole in the wall. Then it was gone.

Was that a way out, Fergal wondered. A means of escape? Maybe. Maybe it was. But he felt sure it would be guarded. D.S. would have thought of that. He wouldn't let anyone get away that easily. Would he?

Still the cans kept coming. They packed them into the boxes and managed to catch up.

"Okay? You all right now?"

The box maker nodded and went back to making up the boxes. The process ran on as before, like clockwork, cold, cruel clockwork. There was nothing human about it. This wasn't about machines at the service of mankind. It was mankind, the slaves of machines.

And still the cans kept coming.

Cans, cans, cans.

Fergal looked around the dull, drab surroundings. If he couldn't leave, then how could he get a message out? How could he get help?

The answer was obvious. Others had thought of it before him.

A message in a bottle. The clank of the rollers seemed to sing it.

Message in a bottle.

Message in a bottle.

That was what had brought him here, and that was the one thing D.S. didn't know about.

"How did you get here? What brought you here? Huh?"

Fergal had never said. He'd had the good sense not to reveal that. That line of communication was still secure — unreliable, erratic and unpredictable, and success was not guaranteed. But it was secure.

Message in a bottle, message in a can. But how was he to get a message into one of the cans? Obviously it could be done. It had been done. But where could he get paper from? And something to write with — a pencil, a pen? And supposing he managed to write a message, and supposing he got it inside a can, and supposing that can was smuggled out, nestling in a box, among all the other cans, even supposing that it got out into the world, would anyone ever find it?

Suppose he could somehow sabotage the can, so that its label would come off in transit? So that when the box finally arrived at its destination and was unpacked, and when the shelf stacker went to put the can on the shelf, it would have no label. Or the label would be left lying in the box. And, of course, they weren't going to bother to stick it back on. They'd just throw it away.

Into the bin. And the can would never be opened or seen again.

Or . . .

It would be put into the bargain basket. There it would lie, waiting for the bargain hunters, for the ones who liked to take a gamble, or even for people just like him . . . people who collected cans.

Sad people, crazy people, odd people, not-altogether-fitting-in people, people who were a bit too clever or a bit too daft.

And one of them might buy the can, the strange, lightweight can with no label, and they would take it home and open it up and take out his note, his plea for help, and then . . .

They would throw it into the bin.

Crumple it up, chuck it away. Think it was all a stupid joke. Pay no further attention to it. And that would be the fate of his message in the bottle. Sunk to the bottom. Lost at sea. Colonized by barnacles, strangled by seaweed, swallowed by a shark. And he would never know. He would just go on hoping and waiting and praying and dreaming, and wondering if his message had ever been found. He would go on as he was, shipwrecked and cast away in this awful place, marooned in this ocean of noise and work and endless monotony, with the massive, unconquerable shoals of cans, cans, cans, swimming toward him forever and ever.

Or . . .

They might not throw it in the bin.

There was the possibility; the so slim, so slender, so fine and delicate thread of possibility; the possibility that someone might find it, read it, and believe in it, and be moved to act upon it. Just as Fergal had. Yes. That was what he had to believe in, that was whom he had to put his trust in, in somebody like himself. Someone a little bit unconventional.

Someone like himself. Or Charlotte. Yes, ask for help, but warn them of the dangers, tell them to be careful, very, very careful, so that they didn't become victims themselves.

Only where was he going to get the paper he needed?

He could rip the label off a full can on the conveyor belt, that would give him paper. Only it would also create another label-less can — one more for the bargain basket, which would reduce the chances of any can with a message in it being found. Which would make things even worse.

So where?

Fergal went on packing the cans. As he did, he looked back down the production line. The room went back a long, long way. It was dimly lit and airless, neither heated nor air-conditioned, the kind of place that would be stifling in summer and freezing cold in winter.

At the far end of the room the cans emerged from the filling and sealing area via a hatch in the wall. The sickly sweet smell, which he had at first found nauseating, no longer bothered him. It was part of the background now, like the noise and the stale air.

The silver cans were carried along six abreast, and then were channeled into a narrower conveyor, which took them, one at a time, into the labeling machine.

Gadunksloop!

The sound the labeler made as it wrapped a label around every can. The labels were in a continuous roll and were cut to size and glued on by the machine. And they were made out of paper.

Paper.

There was the paper. If he could just get his hands on it. Paper for a message. Lots of it.

How was he going to do it? The labeler was fifty feet from him. He would have to run there, pull off a length of label paper, and run back. One hundred feet altogether. How long would that take him? Ten seconds, maybe? There and back, plus time to pull a stretch of label paper off and stuff it into his pocket. Ten seconds. How many cans would fall off the conveyor in that time?

Fergal counted. How fast were they coming?

A-one. A-two.

About two a second. Two cans a second. Ten seconds to get there and to come back. Allow fifteen for errors. Fifteen seconds at two cans a second — thirty cans. He would miss thirty cans. It was too many. If thirty cans fell onto the floor and D.S. came by and saw thirty dented cans . . .

No. He couldn't take the risk. He would need help. From where though? The box maker. It would have to be. Fergal had helped him, now he would have to return the favor.

"Xavier!"

He looked up.

"Cover for me."

Xavier didn't understand. His English was poor, almost nonexistent.

"Cover for me."

Fergal mimed a dumb show of what he wanted him to do. The box maker looked panic-stricken, as if he feared that Fergal was asking him to take over both jobs forever, but then he seemed to understand that it was only for a moment. He nodded and got ready.

"Now!"

The box maker took over the can stacking. Fergal ran. He sprinted the fifty feet to the labeler, he'd never run so fast in his life. He did it in seconds. He grabbed at the roll of paper just as the machine went to wrap a label around a can. The cutter narrowly missed his fingers. Instead of the can, it wrapped the label around his hand instead.

He needed more labels. One piece of paper might not be enough. Better to get several. He yanked at the roll again and a length of paper spun off. The cutter bit through it with a decisive chop.

Maybe just one more now, to be on the safe side — if trying to be on the safe side wasn't too much of a risk.

"Fergal!"

Xavier called his name, starting to panic now, afraid that he couldn't cope.

"Coming!"

The arm of the labeler moved back and forth again, and again the razor-sharp cutter sliced at the paper, missing Fergal's fingers by millimeters. It made him think of that fast-food advertisement for takeaway chicken. *Finger-licking good*, the slogan had said. Only this was finger-chopping. Yes, finger-chopping, finger-slicing, finger-dicing bad.

Fergal Scissorhands.

Please no. Not that.

"Got it!"

He ran back, stuffing the paper into his pocket as he went.

"Okay, Xavier. I've got them. Back to the boxes."

They had fallen behind a little, but not by much. The next box wasn't quite ready but Fergal only had to stack about ten cans on the floor before they caught up with the backlog.

"Thanks."

Xavier nodded. Fergal wondered about him. Had he guessed why Fergal had wanted the paper? Did he have any inkling of what he was up to? If he did, would he betray him? Maybe. Maybe not. These were chances you just had to take.

The cans kept coming. Fergal went on putting them into the boxes. Twelve by twelve. One hundred and forty-four. How nice, how very useful, to know your twelve times table.

He reached out and picked up the next in line. Two silver cans, without labels. He quickly put them into the box and hastily closed the lid. He didn't want D.S. coming by and seeing that. He might start asking questions. Fergal pushed the box on down the rollers to the child who taped the boxes. Only when he saw that the lid had been sealed did he feel able to relax. He wondered if the box taper had seen what he had done, and if she might betray him too.

But she, like all the others, looked dull, glassy-eyed, and uninterested, broken in body and spirit by the dull monotony of the factory, by the tyranny of cans.

Fergal had paper. All he needed now was something to write with. And then the chance to slip the message into one of the cans, before it was filled and sealed. After that, he needed the right person to find it, to . . .

"What do you think you're doing?"

D.S. stood in front of him. For such a big man, he was surprisingly quiet. He could creep up on you quite undetected. You would turn, and he would be there.

"N-nothing. Just . . . working."

"Good. Then see you do."

His shirt was white, it looked fresh and neatly pressed. He wore a striped tie around his neck, and to protect his clothes he had on a brown overall coat, which almost came down to his knees.

What was most repulsive about him was his complete and utter respectability, his seeming ordinariness. His hair was cut short and neatly combed, his complexion was florid, his face clean shaven, apart from a small, clipped moustache. He was heavy and over-weight. The only unusual thing about him was his left hand. It lacked a finger. The small finger. The one on which you might wear a signet ring, if you had one, if your name was Jonathan Dimble-Smith.

"Carry on, then," he said. "Just carry on."

"Erm . . . excuse me . . ." Fergal's mouth was suddenly dry. He felt like Oliver Twist asking for more. Though all he wanted was less. "When do we get a break, please?"

D.S. stopped in his tracks.

"A break?"

"Yes. Don't we get a break today?"

"You get a break when you finish."

"But we've been working for hours."

"Then when you've been working for a few more hours, you'll get a break, won't you?"

"But . . ."

"But what?!"

Fergal could see there was no point in continuing.

"Nothing."

"Good."

D.S. gave a small snort, and moved on his way. As he went, Fergal saw something fall from his coat. It rolled toward him. He looked down, and there it was on the floor. It must have dropped from a hole in D.S.'s pocket or from the frayed inner lining.

It was a ballpoint pen. Cheap and ordinary, and costing no more than a few pence. But to Fergal it was worth a small fortune. He hurried to it and picked it up. It was safely in his pocket before D.S. could turn round, take a last look at the packing bay, snort again, and move on.

The cans kept coming. Fergal picked up two more and placed them into a box. Even as he did so, another two were on the way. And another two were following them.

Endless hordes of cans.

15. THE MESSAGE

It was time to take stock. So Charlotte set everything out on the cabinet by her bed. There was little enough there, and none of it would have persuaded even the most trusting adult to take her seriously. Some unlabeled cans. Some codes. A scrap of paper with the word *help* scrawled on it. And that was it. The stud was hidden somewhere in Fergal's room, or maybe it had vanished with him, and the ring had gone with the finger and the ear. They were at the rubbish tip now, with the other contents of the freezer.

There was nobody she could turn to. There was nowhere she could go. There was nothing she could do, except to go on looking, hoping to find some cans in the supermarket that bore the same codes as those on the bases of the unlabeled cans.

She would have to go on looking, and if she was lucky she would eventually find a match . . . just as Fergal must have done. Then, when she had discovered where the cans were coming from . . .

Yes?

Then what?

What would she do then? She didn't know yet. But she would do something. And she'd do it fast.

"Charlotte!" Her mother's voice called up the stairs.

"Yes, Mum?"

"Did you want to come shopping?"

"Yes. Yes, please."

Charlotte grabbed the piece of paper she had with the codes written on it and hurried down the stairs. Her mother was waiting in the hall.

"Mum," she said. "Before we go, can I speak to you a moment about Fergal and about, well — our cans?"

Her mother's face clouded over.

"No, Charlotte, you may not. In fact I would prefer it if you never mentioned cans to me *ever* again. I have had it with cans all the way up to here!"

"But, Mum —"

"And if I have to listen to another single word about them, I'll go mad. So no more silly stories about cans. Please!"

"But, Mum —"

"Charlotte — that'll do! I forbid it."

"Okay, Mum. All right. Never mind."

"Good. Are you ready?"

"Ready."

"Come along, then. Let's get to the supermarket. We've got a lot to stock up on — and all those frozen things to replace as well. We'd better take the cooler with us, to bring the frozen stuff back in."

"Okay."

It was fine by Charlotte that her mother had a lot of shopping to do. It would give her more time to herself, time to work her way methodically along the aisles, upturning cans, looking for codes, hoping to find a match. And hoping to find Fergal.

But she didn't. Not that day. She did her best and as much as she could, but she didn't match the codes up, and there were still aisles and aisles to cover when her mother came and found her and told her that it was time to go home.

She would have to leave it to another day. Another precious day. And, in between, more precious days of time slipping by, and what did that mean for Fergal and for whoever had written the note asking for help? Where were they? Were they afraid? Were they wondering what she was doing to help them? Were they wondering, during every minute of every hour, if this would be the day when Charlotte would come — Charlotte, their only hope, their only friend.

Tick. Tock. The seconds went by in long slow sweeps, moving more like a scythe than a pendulum, mowing the minutes, cutting them down. There were great swathes of time to get through before the next weekend would come and Charlotte could go to the supermarket again to search for the can that would give her the clue she needed.

Numbness settled over her. What should she do? What could she do — but keep looking, as much and as often as she could. Midweek, after school: She sneaked off to the shop at every opportunity and worked her way along the rows of cans.

Same as ever, the following Saturday morning Charlotte and her mother went to the supermarket to do the week's shopping. Again Charlotte searched the aisles, again she failed to find anything with a similar code, again her mother came to fetch her, the trolley overflowing, telling her that it was time to go.

With a heavy heart Charlotte followed her toward the checkout. As they went, they passed the bargain basket. All the usual suspects were there: bashed cereal boxes and unpopular products nobody wanted to buy.

And a can. A shiny, bright can. Without a label. She reached out in passing and picked it up. It was lighter than she'd expected. She shook it. It didn't rattle, it more fluttered, as if it contained a small, palpitating heart. Or as if there was a rolled-up ball of paper inside.

"Charlotte!"

"Coming!"

She hurried to the till, the silver can grasped tightly in her hand.

"Mum, can you lend me the money for this? It's not much."

"Oh, Charlotte — don't you have enough of those? They clutter your room up terribly."

"Just one more, Mum. Just one more."

"Oh, I don't know . . ."

"If you let me have my pocket money, I'll pay for it out of that."

"Oh, I suppose so. Go on, then."

"Thanks, Mum."

"But make this the last."

Charlotte didn't promise that. It wouldn't have been the last if others had been necessary. Only, as it turned out, it *was* the last. It held the key to everything.

Charlotte turned the can over and inspected the printed code on its base.

It matched.

As soon as she got home, Charlotte took the can up to her room and opened it. She shook its contents out on to her desk. A wodge of labels fell out. There were several of them, rolled up like banknotes. Charlotte flattened them out and studied them.

Dimble-Smith's Premium Dog Food the top label read, and so did the next one, and the one after that. There was a picture of a happy-looking dog wagging its tail as it tucked into a bowlful of what could only have been Dimble-Smith's Premium Dog Food itself.

Charlotte looked again at the code on the bottom of the can. DFBN256 101190 03:01 AO.

Things were starting to make sense now. If BN meant Batch Number, then maybe DF stood for Dog Food.

She picked the wodge of labels up. She looked at the first one closely. In small print at the bottom there was the manufacturer's name and an address and the words, "If not fully delighted by and satisfied with this product, please write to: Customer Relations, Dimble-Smith Foods Ltd., The Barn, Barn Road, Havverstock."

Havverstock? That was near where she lived. Just ten or fifteen miles distant, out in the country, a short bus ride away.

She turned the label over. Writing covered the back of it, and the back of the next label — in fact, the backs of all of them. It was tiny writing, in a neat, if somewhat unusual and slightly eccentric-looking, hand. It was as if the author had had a lot to say, and not much space to say it in. Each label was numbered from one to twenty.

Charlotte thought of the first message that she and Fergal had found: that one scrawled word *help* on the little piece of paper. Compared to that, this was an essay — not a mere cry for help, but a great, long wail.

But the biggest shock of all came when she found label one and began to read what was written.

It was a letter, addressed personally, to her.

Dear Charlotte, *it began*. Or maybe you are not Charlotte. I have a feeling that it will be you, Charlotte. Call it a sixth sense, if you like. But if I am wrong, and you are not Charlotte who is reading this, well, whoever you are, please help me anyway. I am in awful, terrible trouble and have nowhere else to turn. You are my only hope. I am just a child and have been trapped and held prisoner, along with other children even more unhappy and unlucky than myself. At least I have a mum and dad who I know are looking and searching for me and grieving for me and who will never give up until the day they have found me. But some of the other children here don't even have parents. Some do, but their parents believe them to be happy and well looked after. They even have to write letters home to tell them that, although not a word of it is true.

We're all held prisoner, every one of us. We are never allowed outside and all we do is work and sleep, work and sleep. The food we get to eat looks and smells like the food we make: dog food and cat food. (And there's not much difference between them.)

I realize that people think that things like this don't happen today. They know that maybe in some other countries children are treated like slaves and forced to work from when they are only a few years old, but they say it could never happen here. Well, it does.

I found the code, you see, Charlotte. I matched it up in the supermarket. So yes, I found it, and I should have waited for you, only you were away on holiday and I just couldn't be patient enough. I kept thinking of the severed finger and the note saying *help,* and I thought someone could be in awful danger, so I felt that I couldn't delay. I had to help them immediately.

So I set off alone. My parents thought I was going to the library. But really I got the bus out to Havverstock, to find the factory.

It really is in the middle of nowhere. The bus lets you off and you have to walk a good mile or more to get to it. It's surrounded by a fence made of barbed wire. I had to climb over it and I cut my hands and almost tore my fleece to shreds.

The first thing to hit you is the smell. It's like that awful smell you get from factory farms, where they keep pigs and chickens all locked up in sheds without sunlight or any fresh air. Once you smell that smell, you never forget it.

The factory is not very large, not as factories go. It is housed in a few old buildings, cold and drafty. In the yard there is a truck and two trailers with DIMBLE-SMITH written on the side. Once I was over the fence, I was careful not to be seen, because I kept remembering about the severed finger and the severed ear and the note and I was more than a little bit afraid. I maybe wished I hadn't come on my own and had waited for you, or told a grown-up.

Only by then it was too late.

I crossed the yard. There didn't seem to be anybody about, but I could hear the noise of machinery coming from the main building. I made my way to it and tried to see in, but all the windows had been painted over in white paint, and they were covered with steel bars and metal grilles too.

I moved along the side of the building until finally I found a window where some of the paint had weathered away. I put my eye to it and peered inside. And guess what I saw? Everyone working there, all the people manning the machinery and operating the production line, was a child. Some were maybe no more than five or six years old. And there they were, being forced to make dog food and cat food, to work on the conveyor belts, to use all the lethal-looking machinery.

It wasn't just the canning process that looked deadly either; there was all the preparation too: putting offal and waste meat into a big hopper with huge sharp blades that churned it all up until it was fine enough to be flash-cooked and then piped into the cans.

I couldn't believe my eyes at first. I just couldn't. But I knew straightaway that it was all so very wrong. So I turned to go, to run away and get help as fast as I could, only when I did . . . I ran straight into the hands of a woman. She was big and strong and thin-lipped. She looked like the sort of woman who didn't like children — nor anyone else much either.

She got me by both arms and I screamed and kicked and struggled. I really did fight as hard as I could, but she was just bigger and stronger than me. And soon a man came to help her, and between them they managed to hold me still. They turned out my pockets and they took my mobile phone.

There is something I have to tell you about them, about this man and this woman. He has only four fingers on his left hand, whereas she has most of her right ear missing, though she tries to disguise it with her hair.

"Who are you?" the man said. "What are you doing here? What do you want?"

I tried to bluff it and pretend to be all innocent.

"Nothing," I said. "I'm just lost. I was out for a walk with my mum and dad and . . ."

They looked a bit worried when I said that, when I mentioned my mum and dad.

"Where are they, then?" the man said, turning to the woman. "I've not seen anyone. Have you?"

"No," the woman said. "He's lying. He's here on his own."

"I'm not," I said. "We were out for a walk. They'll be by any minute."

"Why did you climb over the fence?"

"I didn't, I was just . . . looking around."

"What were you looking in the window for? What did you see?"

"Nothing," I lied.

"Yes, you did. So you'd better tell me. What did you see in there?"

"Nothing, no one, nothing at all."

The woman turned to the man.

"We can't let him go," she said.

"Yes, you can," I said.

"Too risky," she said.

"No, it isn't," I told her.

"He might have seen something."

"I've not seen anything."

But they weren't listening to me.

"You're right," the man said. "We can't chance it."

"But I didn't see anything!" I insisted.

"So what are you doing here? Eh?"

"I'm just interested," I said, as innocently as possible, "in cans."

I definitely shouldn't have said that. The man sort of smiled when I did. It was a very unpleasant smile too.

"Interested in cans, are you?" he said. He held his hand up so that I could see he had a finger missing. "They can be dangerous things, you know, cans. Very sharp and dangerous. It's all too easy to injure yourself in a canning factory. I speak from bitter experience. Don't I, my dear?"

The woman gave a grim, rueful smile.

"Don't we both?" she said.

And her hand went up to her hair, to where it hung in bunches, by her missing ear.

"Yes," the man said. "Very sharp and dangerous things, cans. Especially when you're working with old machinery. Health and safety regulations, you see, very expensive to implement. They could easily put an honest man out of business."

"Bureaucracy, red tape . . ." The woman nodded.

"So we find," the man said, "that it's all best left to children. Because if they go having accidents, cutting their little fingers off, or chopping off their hands or their feet or their dear little noses, or if they go falling in the hopper and getting turned into dog food, well, that doesn't matter, does it? Because nobody's going to miss them."

I knew by then that they weren't going to let me go. If I hadn't known too much before they had started telling me, I did now.

"So, if you're interested in cans," the man said, "you've come to the right place. Because we're looking for youngsters who are interested in cans. A good career awaits them here. In fact everything you do from now on will be devoted to cans. You'll be able to spend the rest of your life with them. How does that suit you? Come on! Move it!"

Well, I bit and kicked and scratched as hard as I could, but I was overpowered and taken inside. I heard the door clang shut behind me and the sound of a double lock. And I've not really seen daylight since. All I've done is work.

There are two shifts here — all day and all night. We have to work twelve hours at a stretch and we're lucky to get a break. It must be the worst, most tedious job in the world to work on a conveyor line and to do the same task over and over and over again. You have to do it until all your muscles ache and your mind goes numb.

When we get to sleep, we're cramped together into two small rooms — one for girls, one for boys. Sometimes you have to wake somebody up to tell them that it's time for them to go to work so that they will get out and you can have their bed. The food we get is disgusting. Mr. and Mrs. Dimble-Smith look pretty well fed though. Mr. Dimble-Smith insists that we call him D.S. and we have to call her Mrs. D.S., and if you don't, you get a whack round the ear. D.S. has an awful temper and is always shouting. If you drop a can and put a dent in it, or slow down the production line in any way, he goes mad, as if you're trying to rob him.

I found out what happened to his finger. Apparently there was a blockage in the hopper. He refused to turn the machinery off though, as that would have meant shutting down the production line. He doesn't care about safety as much as he does about money. There are no safety guards anywhere on the machinery. You could so easily lose a limb or even fall in and be turned into mincemeat.

Anyway, he tried to free the blockage with a piece of metal and when that didn't work he just reached in and yanked it out, losing a finger in the process. And believe it or not, all he did was laugh — at losing one of his own fingers! He went round the factory waving the bleeding stump at everyone and saying things like, "This is what'll happen to you if you don't work harder! This is what you'll get!" Angelo told me.

Angelo and Xavier are brothers. Angelo's English is better, but Xavier is trying to learn. They come from Eastern Europe. The Dimble-Smiths adopted them from an orphanage there and promised them a better life, but all they got was this pet-food factory and work all day long.

Some of the children are from Africa, others from Asia. The Dimble-Smiths go and find poor families and get friendly with the parents. They tell them that they will pay for the children to come and live with them here, that the children will go to good schools and get a proper education and so will have a better future than they could ever expect at home.

The Dimble-Smiths have a foreman, Leonard Miller, who looks after the place while they are away. I haven't seen much of him, as he seems to spend most of his time sitting in his office, muttering and swearing and drinking bottles of whisky. You always know when he's finished one as you can hear it breaking as he chucks it across the room. Now and again he patrols around the factory and shouts at you to work harder. I think he's a kind of slave too really; he's a slave to whisky, and to the Dimble-Smiths who buy it for him. I daresay he might like to escape as well, but doesn't know how to either. Mr. Dimble-Smith is the only one allowed to drive the truck and to make the deliveries to the supermarkets.

I don't know how Mr. Dimble-Smith's finger ended up in a can — well, in a can on its own. The filler can be a bit erratic sometimes. Just as we suspected, there is no quality control and all the cans are packed straight into boxes after labeling, without any further checks.

Exactly how Mrs. Dimble-Smith lost her ear I don't know either, and I certainly wouldn't dare ask her, as she'd bite your head off. But I guess it must have been the hopper too. For safety you're supposed to have your hair tied up or under a white paper hat. I know, because I saw a notice on the wall saying so. Maybe years ago somebody else owned the factory and it was run properly. Mrs. Dimble-Smith's hair is very long. I can only imagine that she got pulled into the machinery by her hair and lost most of her ear before Mr. Dimble-Smith bothered to stop the machinery by hitting the emergency button.

They wear their injuries a bit like badges. The way Mr. Dimble-Smith points at you, it is as if to say, "See that? I've lost a finger and I don't even care. And if I don't care about that, think how much less I care about you, and what might happen to you. Just remember it, and don't cross me."

Only what might happen to us, Charlotte? As we grow up and get bigger? Because, you see, there's no one here much older than I am. Only why not? I kept asking myself that. I asked Angelo too.

I said, "Why do you think that is, Angelo?" He gave me a look as if I was a bit stupid and had led a sheltered life — which I have done, I suppose, compared to him.

"Why aren't there any older children, Fergal?" he said. "Why do you think?"

"I don't know. Really."

"Because when children get older they get bigger and stronger. They're better able to answer back and to fight back. And Dimble-Smith wouldn't want that. That's why he brings only young children here, ones too small and too afraid to fight.

"But they must grow up. They must get older. Even with the rotten food here and the lack of daylight. They must get bigger."

"I'm sure they do," Angelo said.

"So what happens to them then?" I asked him.

He gave me a look of pity then. It was strange. Because there he was, an orphan, far from home, turned into a slave. He had nothing in the world except his brother and the awful Dimble-Smiths. He had been tricked and deceived, yet he felt sorry for me.

"What do you think happens to them, Fergal?" he said. "What do you think? Now, excuse me, I'm exhausted, and I have to go to sleep."

So he went to sleep on the bottom bunk of the bunk beds in the room we all share. But I stayed awake, wondering what he meant, listening to the sounds of the factory, the drone and rattle and clanging of the conveyor, the high-pitched whine of the hopper and the sound of the mixer, as its blades whirled round and round, cutting up and pulverizing the meat into pet food.

Then I knew.

I knew, Charlotte, what happened to children when they got older, when they started to get big enough to become a threat. They had a little accident. They tripped over the edge of the slicing machine and into the very mincer itself. There's no safety rail, nothing at all. It could happen all so easily. All it would take would be a nudge or a push, a trip or a fall.

And it would all be over.

And no one would know. They'd never know. You'd hardly even know yourself. Then along you'd go, to be flash-cooked and steamed with everything else, and the next thing . . .

You'd be in a can, Charlotte.

You'd be in a can.

I'm the oldest here. And the biggest. The others have all been here so long they are malnourished, but not me. I've caught Mr. Dimble-Smith giving me looks, wondering maybe if I'm already too much of a risk to him. Or maybe he's afraid that someone will come looking for me; he's afraid of prying eyes and awkward questions, of anyone coming anywhere near his factory. And of course, he would be, because if anybody ever found out what he was doing here, they'd lock him away forever.

Which is maybe why he dresses so respectably, and always wears a crisp white shirt and a nice tie. So that when he goes outside nobody will suspect. They probably all think he's that nice, kind, quiet Mr. Dimble-Smith, who always puts five pounds into the collection plate and who keeps himself to himself, and how sad it is that he had an accident and lost a finger.

How little they know.

You've got to help me, Charlotte. Or if it's someone else reading this, please, you've got to help. I'm taking a terrible risk in writing this. If D.S. catches me with this letter in my pocket, I'm as good and as bad as dead.

I'm going to try to send it this morning. It's my turn on the filler.

The empty cans come along, and the cooked and chopped-up pet food is squirted into each one from an overhead tube, which leads from the hopper. Then the filled can goes on to be sealed with a lid and wrapped with a label. I have to pull a handle to release the right amount of dog or cat food (it's basically the same stuff, they just change the labels) into each can. It's the sort of job a robot could do.

Putting my letter into an empty can will be the easy bit. I just pick out a can, put the letter in, and don't pull the lever to fill it with pet food.

But here comes the tricky bit.

If I want my can to end up in a bargain basket and for there to be any hope of you, or somebody like you ever finding it, Charlotte, I have to make sure that it doesn't have a label. See?

But I've got a plan. It's taken me ages to work it out. I thought I was going to have to leave my post and keep my eye on the can, all the way to the wrapping process, and then run and pull the label off it.

Only, if I did that, I wouldn't be pulling the handle to fill up the cans. By the time I got back, loads of cans would have gone through, all empty, all with nothing at all inside them. And if D.S. had discovered that . . . I'd be mince.

Then I got it.

So simple.

The answer was in the pet food.

When you fill the can, in each one there's a certain amount of jelly — oily meat jelly. So this is what I have to do — simply smear my can with a small amount of the jelly, and then it will be so greasy that the glue won't stick.

And neither will the label.

I think it'll work. I'm pretty sure it will. In fact, thinking about it all took my mind off the misery for a while. It was a bit like working out a chess problem or solving a Sudoku puzzle.

If you get this letter, Charlotte, whatever you do, DO NOT COME HERE ALONE. You must tell someone — my mum and dad, your mum and dad, the police, anyone who will listen. But DO NOT COME HERE ALONE UNDER ANY CIRCUMSTANCES, or you will end up the same as us — a slave, in a world of cans.

But if you can't make anyone believe you, if they won't come, then stay where you are. Whatever you do, don't come here alone. I would rather end up in a can myself than bring my friend to share my awful fate. So please try to help me, Charlotte, but not at the cost of your own life and freedom. If you never come, well, I guess I will never know if you ever even received this letter. But I think I will go on believing that you did. That somehow you found it, that you tried to help me, that you did the best you could.

Either way, it was nice to know you and to have met someone else who didn't think it was stupid to enjoy collecting cans.

Well, I've run out of labels now. This is my last one. Bye, Charlotte. I hope you find this. Thanks for being my friend.

Your friend in turn,

Fergal Bamfield (Ferg)

P.S. If you see my mum and dad, please tell them that I love them and ask them to change the brambles for my stick insects. Thank you.

It was early evening in the Bamfield house. Mrs. Bamfield had gone up to the bedroom to lie down. She had drawn the curtains and then fallen asleep on the bed.

She had left a note for Mr. Bamfield in the kitchen, to the effect that she wasn't hungry and didn't want to be disturbed. She had added that he should make himself something when he came in, or maybe go round to the chip shop for a fish supper. Failing that, there was plenty of food in the freezer.

Somewhat disappointed at not being greeted with a hot meal on his return from work, Mr. Bamfield went to the garage and inspected the freezer contents. Nothing there much appealed to him. Nether did he feel like getting back into his car and driving for the takeout. He was in one of those moods when he didn't really know what he wanted.

What he really wanted was a surprise. A surprise . . .

Now where would he get one of those?

Quietly, tentatively, he climbed the stairs up to Fergal's room. There everything was, unnaturally tidy, waiting for him to come home.

At first the room had had an air of quiet confidence about it; now, as the days and weeks had gone by, it seemed less certain of its occupant's eventual return.

Mr. Bamfield looked around him; a lump came to his throat. Fergal, poor Fergal . . .

There was Fergal's backpack, there were his books, there was his CD collection . . .

And there were his cans. All shiny and gleaming, just as he had left them.

Mr. Bamfield crossed the room to inspect them. He reached out, selected one at random, and took it from the shelf.

"For you, Fergal," he whispered. "I'll open this one for you."

And he returned to the kitchen.

Mr. Bamfield fetched a plate and the can opener. With solemn ceremony he clasped the butterfly opener around the rim of the can.

He squeezed the handles. The blade cut in. The vacuum broke. He wound the key.

Then the lid was open. Mr. Bamfield prised it up with his finger. He peered at the tin's contents. His nostrils twitched. An expression of mild disgust crossed his face.

He reached for a spoon and disgorged the contents from the can, dumping them out on the plate.

Well, now that really was off-putting.

There was no way he was eating that.

The smell of it alone was enough. Never mind the sight of it — that pinky-gray mushy look it had. It was hard to know exactly what it was supposed to be. It smelled like some kind of economy-brand pet food.

Mr. Bamfield poked the pile of meat with the end of his spoon.

As he did, he heard a clatter and then a long, plangent meow.

He turned to see that Angus the cat had entered through the cat flap and was looking up at him with a quizzical and appealing expression.

"Is that for me?" he seemed to ask. Then his small red tongue came out of his mouth and he slowly licked his whiskers.

Charlotte put the last of the labels down and placed it with the others. She sat awhile, not really knowing what to do. She picked the labels up and shuffled them carefully into order, then she quickly read through everything again; somebody had to do something, and soon. And she was the only one to do it. She was the only one who knew.

She tapped the small stack of labels upon the desk surface, the way you would with a pack of cards; then, holding Fergal's letter firmly in her hand, she left her room and walked downstairs to the kitchen. Her mother was reading a cookbook. Some friends were coming round for dinner that evening, and she was going to make something special.

"Mum . . . ?"

"Yes, dear? What is it? I'm a bit busy. It won't take long, will it?"

"Mum, it's about Fergal . . ."

She looked up from the recipe book in surprise.

"Fergal? Have you heard something about him? Has he been found?"

"Yes and no."

"Yes and no?"

"I mean, he hasn't been found exactly, but I know where he is."

Charlotte's mother looked at her dubiously.

"You know?"

"Yes."

"Where he is?"

"He's in trouble and he needs help. And he's not the only one. There's others as well."

"But how . . . how do you know, Charlotte?"

Charlotte held up the wodge of labels with the small, neat writing upon them.

"I've had a letter. Fergal sent me a letter."

Charlotte's mother looked even more perplexed.

"Sent you a letter? I really don't see how, dear. I picked the post up from the mat this morning, and there was nothing there but circulars and bills. I didn't get any letters, nor did your father, and I certainly don't think you did."

"It didn't come by post."

"Then how did it come?"

"In a can."

Charlotte's mother looked at her with exasperation. "Oh, really, Charlotte. Honestly."

She went to open a cupboard and started to get the food mixer out, along with some pots and pans and bowls.

"But, Mum . . ."

"In a can. Really, Charlotte. A can!"

"It's true, Mum. It was in the can I got this morning. The one I found in the bargain basket, the one without a label."

"Charlotte, don't you think this has gone quite far enough . . ."

"But, Mum . . ."

"This absurd hobby of yours. And now these ridiculous fantasies. It's bad enough having your bedroom half full of the wretched cans. Now we've got this as well."

"But, Mum, it's true. Just read it. It's here, right here, see. Written on the back of these labels. It's from Fergal. It is."

"Yes, Charlotte. Of course it is. Now, if you'll excuse me and get out of my way, I have a dinner party for six to attend to, and it's time that I got started."

"But, Mum, just read it. Please, read it. You'll see for yourself."

"Oh, very well. If I must. If it keeps you happy. But I don't have the time for it right now, Charlotte. Just leave it there and I'll look at it tomorrow. I can't be doing with it now."

"But, Mum, it's true. It's real. It's not a game."

"Well, it sounds like one to me, Charlotte, and I'm sorry, but I can't play along with it right now."

"But, Mum, it's from Fergal, he's been taken prisoner, and there's other children, and they've all been forced to —"

"Charlotte! That's enough!"

Her mother's voice echoed around the kitchen. She rarely shouted, but she had today. Charlotte felt herself go hot, then suddenly cold.

"I've got enough to do, Charlotte. More than enough."

She wasn't going to believe her. She wasn't going to believe.

"I've put up with all I can, Charlotte. All I can and a lot more on top. I've tried to be tolerant. I've tried to put up with your peculiar hobbies and all the rest, but enough is enough."

She wasn't even going to look at the letter. She had pushed it to one side.

"It's almost wicked of you, Charlotte. It really is. When I think of poor Mrs. Bamfield, with her son, Fergal, missing, and everyone looking for him and no one knowing where he is —"

"But I know! I do know!"

"Charlotte, that's enough. Don't interrupt! When I think of poor Mrs. Bamfield and all she must be going through . . . wondering if he'll ever be found . . ."

"But, Mum . . ."

Charlotte's mother ignored her and carried on, thumping bags of flour down on the kitchen counter as she did so, along with rolling pins and stirring spoons and knives.

"When I think of all that family is going through, Charlotte, and when you come down here with your silly, ridiculous stories about letters in cans from poor Fergal himself, well, it just makes me angry with you, Charlotte. It really does. It's just in such poor taste, Charlotte, you know that. You just don't seem to know when or where to stop."

"But, Mum . . ."

"But nothing. That's an end to it, Charlotte. The conversation has finished. Now please take your labels away and let me have the kitchen to myself! I have cooking to do."

"But . . ."

But Charlotte went no further. She could see there was no use. Her mother would not even give her the opportunity to explain or to defend herself. Only it was true about the labels, about the cans, about Fergal being in danger. It was, it was true.

Yet what use was the truth when nobody would believe it, or even listen to it? You were better off with lies. Maybe people preferred to believe lies. Maybe lies were more logical. They made more sense.

"Okay, Mum. All right. I'll leave you in peace."

Charlotte picked up the labels and quietly left the kitchen. A few seconds after she had gone, her mother's anger abated and she turned to say, "I'm sorry, Charlotte, sorry I shouted at you . . . I didn't mean . . . I've just got these people coming round to cook for and . . ."

Only Charlotte wasn't there to hear it. Her mother thought she heard the click of a door from upstairs, as Charlotte went to her room. But she was mistaken. The sound she heard wasn't from upstairs. The door that had been softly closed had not been Charlotte's door. It was the front door. Charlotte had taken her coat and her wallet and, holding the labels tightly in her hand, had slipped out of the house.

Where now?

Who to go to?

She walked briskly on along the street. It was late in the year now, when the nights came early, almost in the afternoon.

Where to? Who to ask? Who would help her? If only her dad had been home. Maybe he would have listened. Maybe. Or there again, maybe not. Maybe he wouldn't have believed her either, or he also would have been too busy to give her his time.

Mrs. Bamfield.

Yes. That was it. Fergal was right. Mr. and Mrs. Bamfield. They would help. They would believe. She would go there at once. They'd tell the police. They'd do something. They'd all go to the rescue. Loads of them, all in force, squad cars and riot vans. They'd drive up there with sirens screaming and lights blazing, and that would be the end of Mr. and Mrs. Dimble-Smith and their horrible factory.

She hurried on. Already the color was fading from the sky. Some cars had put their lights on. There was a big, blood-orange sun on the horizon, slowly dipping down among the winter clouds.

It wasn't far. It wouldn't take her long to get there. Not if she went quickly. Ten minutes, that was all. Fifteen at the most.

"Hello, Charlotte. How are you?"

Who? What? Who had said that? Oh . . .

"Hello, Mrs. Hibberton."

"Hello, Charlotte. Off out on your own?"

For a moment Charlotte wondered if she could tell her, if Mrs. Hibberton would believe her. No. It would take too long. It was far too complicated. To tell the whole story from the beginning, no.

"Just popping to the shops for Mum," Charlotte lied.

"Well, take care, dear."

Mrs. Hibberton walked on, in a hurry to get home probably, before the streets grew dark.

Charlotte continued on her way. She turned a few more corners and took a shortcut she knew along a back lane. Then there she was, on Fergal's street, and then she was outside Fergal's house. She hurried up the path and rang the bell.

Brrrrrrrrrggggg!

The bell rang, but there was no one there.

> *"Is there anybody there?" said the Traveler,*
> *Knocking on the moonlit door.*

Charlotte rang again. Somehow even the sound of the doorbell was eerie, creepy. It reminded her of a poem they had done at school, about a traveler who comes on horseback to an empty, deserted house. He rings at the bell and knocks at the door, but there is no reply. Yet he has the feeling that he is being watched, that there is somebody in there. "The Listeners" — yes. That was the name of the poem, wasn't it? Only were there really listeners, and if there were, who were they? What were they? Ghosts?

Brrrrrrrrrggggg!

Again the empty stillness, again no reply. She pressed the letter box open and called through it.

"Mrs. Bamfield! Mr. Bamfield! It's me, Charlotte! It's about Fergal!"

Nothing. Nobody. No one. Just the cold chill of evening spreading through the streets. Her feet felt leaden, her heart like ice.

"Mrs. Bamfield! It's Charlotte!"

Where had they gone? Maybe they had gone to stay with friends or relatives, Mrs. Bamfield's sister perhaps, not wanting to be alone, waiting and wondering, thinking that each car passing in the street might be a police car, bringing Fergal home. Or worse — bringing the news that Fergal would never be coming home, ever again.

"Mrs. Bamfield!"

"They're not there, love," a voice called from the adjacent house.

Charlotte looked over to see a woman watching her from her kitchen door.

"Do you know where they've gone?"

"To her sister, I think. They asked me to feed the cat."

"Would you know her address?"

"No, sorry, love."

"When will they be back?"

"Couldn't tell you that either. They've had some trouble, you see. Bad trouble. Their boy, Fergal, about your age . . ."

"Yes, I know."

"Ah, I see . . . friend, eh?"

"Yes."

"Well, I can take a message and pass it on when they get back."

Charlotte hesitated.

"No, it's all right. Thanks all the same."

Charlotte retraced her steps back along the path toward the gate. The neighbor watched her go and only went back into her kitchen and closed the door behind her when Charlotte was nearly at the corner of the street.

She walked on, not knowing quite where she was going, but needing to keep moving to keep the cold at bay. It was night now. It wasn't even five o'clock, but already it was night. The street was a stream of headlights and slow-moving cars.

Who to turn to? Where to go? Who would believe you when nobody believed you? Who would believe a child with an incredible story? A story of cans and messages and severed fingers and ears and rings and studs and notes asking for help and sad children from faraway places exploited and abused? Nobody believed children who told stories like that.

"You and your stories! You've gone too far this time, Charlotte."

She could hear the doubts and rebukes and the incredulities echoing in her head.

Charlotte found herself outside the police station. She steeled herself, then walked in. She entered through the main doors and followed a sign to a desk marked INQUIRIES. The inquiries area was all caged in behind toughened glass, just like the desks in a bank or a post office, or any place where people handled money or were at possible danger from members of the public.

Like her.

She rang the bell that said Ring for Attention.

A policeman looked up from some paperwork he was doing in a back room adjacent to the inquiries area. He saw Charlotte's face, raised an eyebrow, finished the sentence he was writing, then slowly and heavily made his way over to the desk. He spoke to her via a small microphone set into the protective glass barrier.

"Help you?"

It was difficult to know where to start.

"I . . . I've found something."

"Lost property, is it?"

"No. In a can."

"A can?"

A look of world-weariness came over the policeman's face; it was a look which seemed to say, "I thought I'd heard it all and I thought I'd seen it all, but here's a new one I've neither heard nor seen before, and I don't much want to either."

"Yes. It's a letter I found in a can. It's from a friend of mine — you know, Fergal Bamfield, the lost boy."

The policeman sighed.

"Lost boy?"

"Yes."

"He's a lost boy?"

"Yes!"

"What, this is like in Peter Pan, is it, love? Peter Pan and Wendy and the Lost Boys?"

"No! No! You must know about him! Fergal Bamfield. He went missing. Everyone's been looking. His mum and dad are frantic."

"Yes, I know, love. I understand. And it's very good of you to be concerned and to offer to help, but we're all doing everything we can and I don't think there's much one small girl can do to help now. Do you?"

"But I know where he is!"

"And where might that be, love?"

"In a factory!"

"A factory?"

"Making cans — well . . . filling cans."

"Cans? I see."

"It's all here. In the letter."

"The letter?"

Charlotte took the can labels from her coat pocket and pushed them under the grille.

"The one I said about. That I found in the can."

The policeman picked up the labels, flicked through them, then pushed them back toward her.

"Look, love," he said, "I'm sure you mean well. I've got kids myself, see, and I know what you're all like. They get fantasies, don't they? I used to get them too when I was your age. Dreams about being a hero, about saving people from drowning and getting medals and being modest about it and all the rest. Am I right?"

"Please, just read the letter. I'm not making it up. He's a prisoner. In the factory. He is!"

But the policeman wasn't listening, not to her — only to himself.

"Of course I'm right. In fact, it was these fantasies I had as a kid that probably made me want to become a policeman — though it's not all excitement in the police force, I have to admit. So look, love, we appreciate your concern. But it's best to leave these things to the authorities. So you take your story that you wrote on the back of the labels here —"

"But I didn't write it. It wasn't me. It was in the can."

"That's right, love. It was in the can. So you take your letter and you take it home and put it back in your can and you keep it nice and safe there. And one day, when you're grown up, you'll look back and you'll remember what you did, and you'll maybe give a little wry smile. We all do, see. We all do."

"But you don't understand . . . !"

Charlotte was almost in tears — tears of sheer anger and frustration. Why wouldn't anyone believe her? Why wouldn't anybody listen?

"You run along then, love. You get home now before it gets too dark or your mum and dad will be wondering. And one lost person is quite enough, isn't it? We don't want another one. So you hurry along now. Or maybe you'd like me to get an officer to take you home. It won't be any trouble, though you might have to wait a few minutes. I can get a woman Police Constable. How's that, now? How would that do?"

Charlotte felt panic rise inside her. That was the last thing she wanted. She couldn't possibly go home, especially not with a police escort — not now, not yet, not while Fergal was still in peril and danger and at the mercy of the vile, vicious Dimble-Smiths. Once home, she'd never be allowed out again, and the more fuss she made about how she knew where Fergal was, the less she would be believed, and the angrier everybody would get with her.

"I'm all right, thank you," Charlotte said. "I can manage to get home on my own. I don't live far away. Thank you all the same."

"Just wait a moment, miss," the policeman began. "Just hold on there. What did you say your name was? Where is it you live?"

But she was already out of the door, stuffing the labels back into her pocket and keeping her hand tightly around them, not letting them out of her grasp.

She ran down the steps and hurried away from the police station, off into the crowd on the high street. People passed her by with shopping bags and carrier bags in their hands. A child, walking alongside his father, was clutching a box of Christmas crackers. The sight startled her. Was Christmas that near? So near that people were already buying crackers and tinsel? Surely there were weeks and weeks to go yet.

Charlotte let her feet guide her. She didn't know exactly where she was going, but she knew that she wasn't going home. How could she go home, when Fergal was waiting for her, for help to come, not knowing if his letter had even been found or if help was on the way.

Mr. Dimble-Smith wouldn't be buying any crackers, that was for sure. Christmas would be a day like any other for the unfortunate souls in his factory. It would be just another day full of cans — and there wouldn't be any Christmas treats in them.

She was at the bus depot. She felt her feet take her to the information point; she heard her voice say, "Excuse me, where can I get a bus to Havverstock?"

"Bay number seven, dear. Goes in three minutes. So hurry over there. It won't hang about."

Then her feet were walking again and her body was squeezing its way through the small army of bag-laden shoppers anxious to get on the buses to take them home.

"Is this the Havverstock bus?"

"Yes, love. It is. Single or return?"

"Oh . . . er . . ."

Look on the bright side, Charlotte, she told herself. *Look on the bright side and let's assume that you'll be coming back.*

"Return, please."

"Return it is, then."

She took out her wallet and paid for the ticket. She had just enough to cover it, and a little to spare. She walked toward the middle of the bus and sat by the window. There weren't very many people going to Havverstock. Maybe three or four, that was all.

The bus started up and pulled out of the depot. It joined the flow of traffic heading out of town. Its diesel engine roared and throbbed. It seemed to start off a repetitive tune in her head, a tune that wouldn't go away, and another part of her mind put words to it, then another part put a voice to the words. It was Fergal's voice, and she could hear him singing, over and over.

"Whatever you do, don't come here alone, Charlotte.

Please, please, don't come here alone."

She tried to make the voice go away, but the dull thud of the diesel kept bringing it back.

"Don't come here alone, Charlotte.

Please, please, don't come here alone."

And what was she doing?

I know, Fergal, I know, I know, I know.

But what choice do you have, when you are just a child, and nobody believes you?

"Don't come here alone, Charlotte. Don't come here alone. You must tell someone — my mum and dad, your mum and dad, the police, anyone who will listen. But whatever you do, Charlotte, do not come here alone, or you will end up the same as us — a slave, in a world of cans."

I tried, but they wouldn't help me, Fergal. They wouldn't listen, they wouldn't believe. I tried.

"Then if you can't make them believe you, if they won't come, then stay where you are. Whatever you do, don't come here alone."

I have to, Fergal, I have to.

"I would rather end up in a can myself than bring my friend to share my awful fate."

I'd rather end up in a can too, Fergal, than have to live knowing that I didn't even try to help my friend.

"Just don't come here alone, Charlotte, that's all. Please, Charlotte, whatever you do, DO NOT COME HERE ALONE!!"

"You on your own, love?"

"Sorry?"

The elderly lady in the seat behind was smiling at her and proffering a bag of sweets.

"On your own, love?"

"Er . . . yes. But there's someone meeting me at the other end."

"That's good — I was going to say. You don't want to be going places on your own on a dark night like this. Would you care for a mint humbug to keep you warm?"

"Thank you. Thank you very much."

Charlotte realized that it must be teatime and her stomach was empty. She sucked the sweet, but she didn't feel hungry really. There was something else filling her stomach, other than the empty pang of hunger: It was fear.

When she got there, what was she going to do? How was she going to do it?

Never mind. Get there, then decide. One thing at a time. And whatever you do, don't get caught. But for now, just turn your mind off, and let the bus take you there, let the time go by.

"Havverstock! I said Havverstock! Oi! You! The girl there! Didn't you want Havverstock? Because we're here."

Charlotte got to her feet and hurried to the front of the bus. The driver revved the engine impatiently, waiting for her to get down. The old lady with the mint humbugs had already gone; she must have got off at an earlier stop.

"Thank you. Sorry. I must have been daydreaming." Only it was dark. Night-dreaming, maybe.

"Okay."

The driver waited for her to go down the steps. She hesitated.

"I don't suppose you know where Barn Road is?"

The driver pointed to a crossroads, just ahead of the bus.

"That's it, love. There on the left. Now I do have a timetable to keep to . . ."

"Sorry," Charlotte said.

She jumped down from the step. The door closed behind her and the bus went on its way.

She was alone in the still of the night.

17. ALL THE ROBOTS

Havverstock was barely a village. It was a small and isolated place with a church, a shop, a few houses, a telephone box, and a crossroads. There was a dried-up duck pond near the graveyard, with an old, ruined stocks by it.

Charlotte reached into her pocket and felt for her phone. It wasn't there. It must have fallen out when she had been running. She stopped by the telephone box. Maybe she ought to call, to tell someone where she was, just in case. But then she realized that the few coins she had were of no use; the payphone only took silver. She didn't even think to call collect. She just hurried on.

Her parents would have noticed that she was missing by now.

Her mum would be up in her room, wondering where she had gone.

It would ruin the dinner party.

If only somebody had listened to her. If only.

She came to the crossroads and took the turn to the left. A faded road sign named the way. ARN R AD, it read. The B of BARN and the O of ROAD were so faint as to be unreadable.

She walked on. It was a cold but clear country night. Pale moonlight showed the way. Her footsteps echoed and seemed at times to be pursuing her, then at other times to be slightly ahead of her, as though she was following them. Hedges and brambles lined the fields, and twisted thorn trees writhed as if locked in pain. A faint, whispering breeze blew, full of murmuring. Distant cattle lowed and the sheep on the hills bleated to each other, like babies crying.

There was the sound of an approaching car. She hid in some bushes. The vehicle came toward her. Its lights were high. Not a car then, probably a Jeep or a Land Rover or maybe a small truck with the words DIMBLE-SMITH & CO., PREMIUM PET FOOD on the side, and Dimble-Smith himself at the wheel. She was momentarily dazzled. She tried to blink the brightness away so as to make something out of the vehicle. But all she could see were its retreating rear lights, glowing red in the darkness, then disappearing around the corner.

"Is there anybody there?" said the Traveler.

No one now. Nobody at all. Just Charlotte, walking on alone, in the deep, country darkness. She stumbled into a ditch and had to extract her foot from a slop of mud. There was a *glug* as she pulled it out. She walked on, her foot cold and wet, but she barely noticed.

She must have walked two miles when finally she came to a turn. There was a narrow track running off to the left, and at the entrance to it was a cattle grid. A rotting wooden nameplate bore the words THE BARN, which seemed to have been branded into the wood. It was secured to a gatepost with twisted wire. There was no mention of any factory. Maybe Mr. Dimble-Smith was concerned not to advertise its presence — for obvious reasons.

Charlotte made her way carefully over the cattle grid, anxious not to slip between the bars and twist a foot or an ankle. She walked on. After a few yards she left the track, climbed over a stile, and walked on along a footpath, where a high hedge shielded her from view.

It proved to be an unnecessary precaution.

"Is there anybody there?" said the Traveler.

No one. No one at all.

"Tell them I came, and no one answered,
That I kept my word," he said.

That was important too, wasn't it? To keep your words and promises, to do what you had said you would. People might be waiting, people might be wondering, relying and depending.

You might be the only hope they had.

"Anybody there?" said the Traveler.

Yes. There was. At least there was certainly something, if not somebody: An obnoxious smell wafted over on the breeze.

Charlotte held her nose. Then she let go and took a deep breath. After a few lungs full, the smell didn't seem quite so nauseating.

She stood and listened. Yes, there it was now. The faint dull drone of machinery; the distant rattle and the muffled sound of what could only be . . . cans. Cans in motion. Cans on their way.

Then she heard a voice. It warbled tunelessly, singing some old-fashioned air embellished with occasional drunken curses. The singing stopped. The brief lull was followed by a crash and the sound of breaking glass, as though a bottle had been hurled into a large, empty bin.

Charlotte remembered Fergal's letter. It must be the Dimble-Smiths' foreman, Leonard Miller, she thought, flinging an empty whisky bottle away before going back inside to start on the next.

She waited, giving him plenty of time to get back in before she peered out from behind the hedge.

There it was. There were the ramshackle buildings Fergal had described, surrounded by the barbed-wire fence. From the top of the fence some fragments of cloth fluttered. Remnants of Fergal's fleece, perhaps.

Inside the compound bounded by the fence were some vehicles — a truck, a van, and a couple of cars. The cars looked new and well polished. The Dimble-Smiths obviously lived well.

At a distance from the factory building were a farmhouse and a small cottage. Presumably the Dimble-Smiths occupied the farmhouse and their foreman used the cottage.

Right, Charlotte thought. No going back now. She had come too far. She wished she had told somebody though. She wished she had told somebody where she was going, where they should look for her if she didn't come back.

"You don't listen, Charlotte, do you? That really is your trouble. You live in your own little world. Head in the clouds, you know. Always going your own way and never thinking of consequences."

"Tell them I came, and no one answered,
That I kept my word," he said.

Charlotte was afraid. But that didn't matter. Good to be afraid, she told herself. Stops you from being stupid and getting caught. Fear and pain, you wouldn't want either, but both of them told you something, about danger and disease, that you had to know — even if you didn't want to.

Then she saw him — Dimble-Smith himself. It had to be him, crossing the yard and heading for the farmhouse. He was just as Fergal had said, large and well scrubbed and respectable; his white shirt reflected the moonlight, and she could see his pale-striped tie. Even though the night was cold he hadn't bothered to put a coat on for the short walk from the factory to the house. He was probably going in for his dinner. A good hearty dinner, eaten in a kitchen warmed by a cozy wood stove.

He had two dogs with him, both on short chains, big, mean-looking things with more teeth than brains and more muscle than either. They trotted along beside him, growling and slobbering. Dimble-Smith was probably taking them in for their dinner too. There'd be no shortage of dog food here.

The door to the farmhouse closed behind him, and the yard was silent again, save for the drone of machinery and a vague tinny rattle coming from inside the buildings.

Charlotte waited a few minutes, giving Mr. Dimble-Smith time to get his knife and fork into his hands and to put his feet under the table. Then she crept toward the fence.

There was no alternative than to climb over. She took the route Fergal had taken. The tatters of torn fleece attached to the barbs told her what to avoid. She climbed over the top of the fence unscathed and dropped down into the cobblestone yard.

Now then, what next?

She kept to the shadows, clinging to them closely. She skirted around the perimeter of the yard and came to the first of the outbuildings. She stopped by a door. She tried the handle, but the door was locked. She released her grip and scurried on, keeping low, so as not to be seen from the farmhouse.

All the factory windows were painted over in white, just as Fergal had said, but here and there the paint had peeled and faded and she was able to peer inside.

It was the preparation area, illuminated by flickering fluorescent tubes. An unpleasant, sickly sweet smell escaped from inside. Some children were there, shoveling offal and unwanted scraps of meat into a huge mixer set in the floor. There should have been safety rails in place, but there were none. An error of judgment, a moment's inattention, a slippery patch on the floor, and you would be in there, along with the butcher's castoffs and the abattoir's leftovers, and the great blades of the mixer would be upon you, and you'd be dog meat and cat feed.

Charlotte moved on to another window. There was only a small unpainted area to see through here, no bigger than a coin. But it was space enough for her to realize that she was looking into the foreman's office. There was Miller. He was well into his next bottle of whisky. His feet were on the desk and his head was tilted back and he was drinking directly from the bottle. He took a swig, swallowed, then thumped the bottle down, got unsteadily to his feet, and prepared to go off on his rounds.

Miller left the room. Charlotte moved away from the window. She came to a second door, but that too was locked. She went on around the building and arrived at another window. She peered in through the flecked paint.

Fergal!

There he was.

He stood there at the end of a conveyor, taking two cans at a time and packing them into boxes. It was extraordinary. He looked just like a robot, moving with all the mindless precision of a machine, endlessly repeating the same movement, over and over. Charlotte half expected to see a key in his back for winding him up or a battery plugged into his head.

She had never seen so many cans either. Along they came, silver as a shoal of minnows.

"Fergal!"

She tapped softly on the window, but he didn't hear her. The sound must have been absorbed by the drone of the machines and the rattling of the conveyor.

She knocked on the window again, louder now. He looked up. But it wasn't toward her, it was in another direction.

Miller had entered the packing area. He lurched along. He stopped by each child in the production line and treated them to a few words of derision and a couple of whisky-flavored threats.

Miller came to where Fergal was working. He scowled at him and seemed to be looking for some evidence of slacking, but finding none, he just cursed Fergal for the sake of it, then moved on.

Once he was gone, Charlotte tapped on the window again. Her knock was stronger, louder. Fergal looked around, puzzled. He even looked in her direction, but he couldn't see her; the whitewash on the window blotted her out.

She had to get in. If she could get in, they could get out. Obviously the doors couldn't be opened from the inside, not without a key, or they would all have escaped long ago. But that wouldn't mean you couldn't open the doors from the outside. She'd just have to try them all and see.

She retraced her steps. Miller was back in his office now, sprawled in his chair with the whisky bottle to his lips. He took a swig, put the bottle down, and cradled his head upon his arms, ready for a nap. Within moments, he was snoring.

Charlotte went to retry the doors. They were all locked. She circled the building in a counterclockwise direction until she was almost back at the packing area, when she saw a single door, hidden in shadow. She reached and took the handle.

It turned. It turned all the way around.

The door opened.

But there was no handle on the inside. If she let it close behind her, she wouldn't be able to get out again, not by this route. She too would be trapped. She looked around for something to jam the door open with. She took a large stone from the yard and placed it by the door frame, to stop the door from closing.

Right. Just a few steps forward now . . .

And then she was inside.

Charlotte breathed deeply, trying to stay calm. The noise of the machinery was louder here. She was in a small corridor, adjacent to the packing area. She walked along slowly, silently, apprehensively.

What if Miller should wake from his drunken slumber? What if Mr. Dimble-Smith or Mrs. Dimble-Smith should decide that it was time they left the warmth of their farmhouse kitchen and saw how the factory was getting on? Or if they let the dogs loose?

Then she saw it. There on the wall. A telephone. Just what she needed. She remembered the words in Fergal's letter — *Whatever you do, Charlotte, DO NOT COME HERE ALONE!!*

Which was exactly what she had done. And what was worse was that in her haste and determination to help, she had rashly left no record behind her of where she had gone.

"Dear Mum and Dad, if I am not back by eight o'clock, come looking for me at . . ."

As soon as they discovered that she had gone, that she had meant it, they would have come looking. And then they would have seen all this for themselves. No question about being believed then. No doubts at all.

Should she risk it?

She reached for the phone.

She had to. She had to tell somebody where she was. If she didn't, and she was captured, it would all have been for nothing. She would disappear, just as Fergal had, just as the other children had. She would be the can collector, collected and canned. Canned inside the factory; its contents the children; the roof its lid; and no one in possession of an opener.

Cans. Cans.

And cans within cans, stacked up like Russian dolls.

Charlotte lifted up the handset, put it to her ear, and reached to dial her home number.

But before she could, a voice spoke. There was someone there, right behind her. She swiveled round. Was it Miller? No. Nobody. Nobody there at all. The voice was coming from the handset, from the telephone itself.

"Miller, you drunken sot, is that you? What do you want?"

The voice had to be his — Dimble-Smith's. Charlotte had made a dreadful mistake. It wasn't a proper phone at all. It was just an internal one, linking the factory to the house.

"Miller? Miller! Miller, we've not even finished our dinner here. Can't you manage to . . ."

She put the handset back into the cradle. She could neither move nor think. She felt sick inside. What had she done? She was supposed to be the rescuer, and now she had fallen into the very same trap. Fergal had warned her, and she hadn't paid any attention. She'd been so stupid, so reckless.

"Whatever you do, don't come alone."

Precisely what she had done. And now Dimble-Smith must have a suspicion that something was wrong. Even as she stood there, frozen with fear, he would be rising from the table saying, "I'd just better go and check on that drunken idiot, Miller. He's probably kicked the phone off his desk."

Even now he would be leaving the farmhouse kitchen, crossing the yard, heading for the outbuildings, his white shirt gleaming in the moonlight, his breath visible in the cold night air.

It had to be now. Now or never. She had to move, to act, now, while there was still a chance.

It was like pulling herself out of the mud again.

Come on, come on, come on, Charlotte! Move, move, move!

She couldn't seem to lift her feet. They were rooted in a thick, clinging ooze of fear.

Mr. Dimble-Smith was probably nearing the outbuildings now. He was reaching in his pocket, taking out the key ring with all the keys on it, finding the one that fitted the lock . . .

At last she freed herself from the terror that had held her immobile. And she ran. She ran to the end of the corridor and burst in through the inner door.

"Fergal! Fergal! Fergal! It's me! The back door's open! We can escape if we go now! Come on! Now! Now! Run, run, run!"

He stared blankly at her from across the room. He didn't seem to recognize her. He just went on moving the cans, from conveyor to box, from conveyor to box.

"Fergal!"

Nothing. He went on packing the cans. It was as if he didn't want to do anything else. He was part of the machinery himself now. Part of the production line. There was no life before and no life after. There was nothing else to want, to do, or to be. This was all there was, this was the point of it all — cans, cans and cans.

"Fergal!"

Charlotte was next to him now. She had him by the shoulders and was shaking him hard.

"Fergal! It's me! We've got to go! Now! Immediately!"

He stopped.

A can fell to the floor. Then another. The sound caused the other children working on the production line to look up.

Another can fell. Another.

"Charlotte?"

"Fergal! We've got to go. Now!"

"But . . . but the cans . . ."

They fell, flashing silver in the light. They dropped like water in a waterfall, a small Niagara of cans. The other children stopped work too. The box maker stopped. The label sealer stopped. And the cans went on raining to the floor.

Nobody made any attempt to stop them. Nobody tried to pick them up, to desperately get the system back on course again. They just let them fall.

Thud, thud, thud. Slowly, ineluctably, the cans fell to the floor, one on top of the other, and rolled away.

"Charlotte . . ."

"Fergal . . . we've got to run."

"You came . . ."

"I found your letter . . ."

"I knew it. I knew you would. Only . . ."

"We've got to go, Fergal. I think he knows I'm here. I think he's coming."

"You didn't come alone?"

"I did, I'm afraid I did . . ."

"But you told someone where you were going . . . you left a message . . . a note . . . ?"

"No." Charlotte blushed. "I tried to tell people, but no one would believe me, Fergal. They don't believe you when you're just a child. Nobody ever believes!"

"Miller! Where the blazes are you, you drunken idiot! You booze-filled buffoon!"

A loud voice boomed from somewhere inside the building. It was half muffled by the noise of the machinery, but it sounded loud enough and angry enough all the same.

"He's coming."

"Then let's go."

Thud, thud, thud, thud.

Still the production line didn't stop. The conveyor belt went on moving; the cans dropped from it like tiny bombs. Angelo and Xavier looked from Fergal to the girl, wondering where she had come from and who she was. From where they stood, alongside Fergal, they could hear that D.S. was coming. He'd be angry when he saw all the cans on the floor. But Fergal was just letting them fall. He was making no effort to catch up on the backlog. And if he wasn't going to bother, then why should they?

Let them fall.

Let them all fall down.

Let all the cans go *thud, thud, thud*. Let all the production lines grind to a halt. Let all the robots and the zombies become human again.

Let them.

Thud, thud, thud, thud.

Let them fall and roll away.

"What the devil's going on in here?!"

He stood in the doorway, big, florid-faced and fearsome. He was carrying a walking stick. But not to walk with.

And she stood just behind him, at his shoulder. Prim and proper, purse-lipped and sour, with child-hating eyes buried deep as currants in a snowman's face.

"You! Where did you come from?"

Thud, thud, thud, thud. The cans went on falling. The production line didn't seem to realize that there was no point to it anymore. Its right hand didn't understand what its left hand was doing. It ran on, like a headless chicken, not knowing that it was dead.

"The back door," Charlotte whispered. "It's jammed open."

"Okay. Angelo . . . Xavier . . ." Fergal called.

It was enough to say their names. Their eyes did the rest. They didn't need to be told what to do. All of them, they ran.

"You! Get them! Get back!"

The Dimble-Smiths lumbered after them, through the flood of cans. They stumbled and staggered across the floor, but Charlotte and the three boys were already away, light and nimble. No longer the automatons they had been for so long, but moving fast and free, hopping over the rolling, falling cans, not missing a footstep, heading for the door to the corridor.

A heavy silver missile whistled past Fergal's ear, missing his head by a whisker. If the Dimble-Smiths couldn't catch them, then maybe they could bring them down with a well-aimed can. A second, then a third fell wide. A fourth one caught him a smart, painful blow in the small of the back.

"Ouch!"

It hurt. But it wasn't going to stop him.

Charlotte pushed hard at the door to the corridor. It banged open and she held it wide as Fergal ran through, followed by Angelo, then Xavier. Then she slammed the door shut. Angelo stared at her.

"The others, what about the others?"

"We'll come back for them, Angelo. We've got to get help."

Cans rained against the other side of the door. Dimble-Smith was flinging cans as he came, shouting and ranting.

"Come back here, you little . . ." he yelled. "I'm going to kill you. I'm going to kill you all. . . ."

Mrs. Dimble-Smith lost her balance among some rolling cans and grabbed at her husband for support.

"Watch what you're doing, you dolt!" he yelled at her. "This is no time for ballet dancing. After them! Come on!"

They pushed their way through the swing door. Now they too were out in the corridor.

The children ran. There at the end of the corridor was their escape route — the exit to the outside world. The stone was still in place where Charlotte had left it, jamming the back door open.

A can flew through the air and landed just in front of Fergal. Without stopping, he picked it up and hurled it back as hard as he could. He was rewarded with a loud, "Owwww! My shin!" from Mrs. Dimble-Smith.

He'd got her, and it served her right.

But the Dimble-Smiths were gaining now. They were hurtling down the corridor as if the devil was behind them and cheering them on. They were coming fast behind Fergal and the others, bearing down like wolves, getting nearer with every step. You could hear them panting and snarling; you could all but smell their breath.

"Okay. Go! Go, go, go!"

Angelo ran through the outside door, followed by Xavier and Fergal.

Charlotte went after him — the last out. As the door swung behind her, she went to kick the stone away, so as to let the door slam shut and to stop the Dimble-Smiths from following.

But the stone wouldn't budge. It seemed to be jammed. She crouched down to pull it away and as she did . . .

A hand shot through the gap between the door and the jamb and grabbed her by the wrist.

A hand with a finger missing.

"Oh no, you don't!" She heard Dimble-Smith's voice. "You just leave that right there."

The three fingers and the one thumb tightened their grip. Had there been four fingers, the hand might have been strong enough to hold her. But as it was, she punched at each of the fingers in turn with the knuckles of her free hand. One.

"Ow!"

Two.

"Ouch!"

Three.

"Stop that, you brat!"

The hand lost its grip.

And then Charlotte grabbed at the stone. She yanked at it with all her strength, managed to pull it clear and thankfully, mercifully . . .

The door clicked shut.

Just in time. She heard a howl of rage from the Dimble-Smiths as their fists beat on the door panels.

"Open it! Open the door!" Dimble-Smith yelled.

"It's no use. It doesn't open from the inside!" his wife's sour voice reminded him. "We need to get out the other way."

Out in the yard, in the cold, crisp night, Fergal paused to breathe the air and to savor the taste of freedom.

"We're not away yet," Charlotte reminded him.

The four of them ran for the fence. Up they went, up and over the top. They got scratched and cut, but they barely felt it. Then they dropped down to the other side. From behind them they could hear the sound of the dogs, barking madly in the farmhouse.

"Which way now?"

"To the village. They can't catch all of us. One of us'll make it. As long as one of us gets there."

On they ran. On down the track to the road, through the mud and the moonlight, on along the road, on to the village, to the telephone box, red and cozy and old-fashioned and glowing like a small beacon.

They didn't look back, not once. If they had looked back, well, who knew what they might have seen? Mr. Dimble-Smith, maybe, not two yards behind them. Or no one. Or maybe a river of cans, a rolling river of shiny cans, flowing behind them like the tide coming up the beach.

All four of them huddled inside the phone box, as if it were the safest place in the world.

"I don't suppose you lot have any coins," Charlotte said.

"Just call collect," Fergal suggested, "or simply dial 911. You don't have to pay for that."

Charlotte looked at him. "You have some quite good ideas sometimes, Fergal," she said. "Even if coming out here on your own wasn't one of them."

"Well, look who's talking!" Fergal said. "Though I'm very glad you did come," he had the decency to add. "Thanks, Charlotte."

"My pleasure," she said. "Now, let's ring the operator. I think I'd better call home first."

Charlotte dialed 0. The operator answered. Charlotte explained that she wanted to make a collect call to her home number.

She heard the operator speaking to her father.

"We have a girl who says she is your daughter on the line. Will you accept —"

"Yes, yes, of course!"

He almost bit the operator's head off.

"Putting you through."

"Charlotte, is that you? Where have you been? What have you been doing? Your mother's practically hysterical. And you've absolutely ruined her dinner party. Are you all right? Where are you?"

Charlotte didn't know whether to laugh or cry. "Dad . . . Dad, I'm all right. I'm fine. I'm with Fergal."

"What? Where —"

Charlotte interrupted him. Her voice was serious and urgent now. "Dad, we need help. We need help from somebody who'll believe us."

There was a second's silence. Then she heard her father's voice say, "Go on, then, Charlotte. Tell me."

"And you'll believe me?"

"I'll believe you."

And he did.

He didn't really have much choice.

18. CANNED

They never found them.

They found Leonard Miller all right, drunk and snoring in his office, with a drop still left in the whisky bottle in his hand, which he was sorry he couldn't finish. They took him away in handcuffs, stolidly protesting his innocence, that he never did any harm to anybody and the Dimble-Smiths were all to blame.

Only where were they?

All of their vehicles were still in the yard, and the gate itself had remained padlocked and bolted from the inside. The police had needed to use bolt cutters to get in.

They found the production line still running and a cluster of wide-eyed, hollow-cheeked children sitting watching it.

The labeling machine had run out of paper and the mixer had run out of meat, but the canner went on putting lids on to empty cans, with nothing in them but air, until finally it ran out of lids too, and eventually there weren't any more cans either. The police officer in charge pressed the red button, which brought the production line to a shuddering halt.

A breeze came in through the open door; an empty can rattled along the gangway. It came to a halt by the policeman's feet. He stooped to pick it up. Silence at last. Finally the cans had stopped. They lay immobile, great piles of them on the floor, like casualties of war.

Fergal was reunited with his parents. At first his mother bitterly reproached him (she was so pleased to see him that she couldn't help but criticize).

"This is where it leads to, you see, Fergal," she said. "See where collecting cans led you! You might have been a slave for life!"

Then she calmed down.

"I do hope you'll find another hobby though, Fergal," Mrs. Bamfield implored him. "There must be something else you can take up which isn't quite so dangerous. Something like bungee jumping or hang gliding. Either of those would be a lot safer than collecting cans, I'm sure."

But, as Fergal so rightly pointed out, if he hadn't started to collect cans, what would have become of the children in the Dimble-Smiths' factory? Who would ever have known about them? Who would ever have gone to their rescue if it hadn't been for Fergal and Charlotte and their eccentric hobby of collecting cans?

The children had been taken away and looked after. Those who had homes were reunited with their parents. Those who were orphans were found decent families to live with. The factory was closed down.

But the Dimble-Smiths had gone. How they had gone, where they had gone, nobody seemed to know.

***

Fergal gave up collecting cans.

"There doesn't seem much point now," he said to Charlotte. "Not anymore. I think you and I have got the most out of cans that we're ever likely to get. I don't think anyone will ever find an adventure in a can as good as the one we've had. It's like winning the lottery. You just don't get adventures in cans like that every day. It's just not possible."

"I agree," Charlotte said. "I mean, how often do you find a finger in a can?"

"Or an ear?"

"Or a gold stud or a ring?"

"Or a note saying *help*?"

"Or a letter on the back of some labels?"

"Yes," Fergal reminded her, "a letter saying, 'Whatever you do, do not come on your own.'"

Charlotte blushed.

"Yes, well . . ." she said. "We all do impetuous things. And maybe it's just as well."

They were in a restaurant at the time, eating pizza. Fergal and Charlotte were together at one end of the table; their parents were all talking animatedly and drinking red wine with their meal.

"Well," Fergal said, "I wonder what I'll take up now. What do you think about collecting jars?"

But Charlotte shook her head.

"No," she said, as she finished off her last mouthful of pizza. "No. Not the same. You can see what's inside jars. Where's the fun in that? Where's the mystery?"

"Yes," Fergal had to agree. "I'll think of something."

The waiter came to take their plates away.

"We've got two very clever children here, you know," Mr. Bamfield told him proudly. "Two very clever children indeed!"

"Yes, we have," Charlotte's mother agreed. "Clever *and* courageous, if I may say."

"You'll be reading about these two in the newspapers soon, I wouldn't be surprised," Mr. Bamfield continued.

"I've already heard about it, sir," the waiter said. "It was on the six o'clock news. May I offer my congratulations and desserts on the house for the young people?"

While they waited for the dessert menu to come, Fergal leaned forward a little, and whispered, "Charlotte . . . ?"

"What?"

"What do you really think happened to Mr. and Mrs. Dimble-Smith?"

She gave him a look. She had been wondering the same thing herself. "Wouldn't like to say," she said. "Why?"

"I just wondered."

"About what in particular?"

"It was the way the children were . . . when we got back to the factory, with the police cars and everyone."

"What about them?"

"It was the way they were all so . . . so quiet . . . just sitting there . . . looking at the machinery . . . at the mixer and the hopper. . . ."

"Yes, I saw them. And so?"

"I just thought that maybe they knew something."

"Like what, for instance?"

"Like where Mr. and Mrs. Dimble-Smith had gone."

"Like where, for example, Fergal?"

"Like . . ." He hesitated. His lips were dry. He took a drink of his cola before he answered. "Like . . . in the mixer."

"The mixer?"

"Yes. Just say, with all the cans on the floor, they came running out of the packing section, heading for the other door so as to get outside and follow us, but there were all these cans rolling about everywhere on the floor."

"And?"

"And say they slipped . . . or skidded . . ."

"Or tripped. Or even were . . . pushed . . ."

"I didn't say that."

"Neither did I."

"Yes, you did."

"I was only suggesting."

"Well, I suppose it's possible. Those children had every reason to hate them. I mean, I'm certainly not saying they did push them. It would have been quite easy to just fall into the mixer. There wasn't a safety guard on it, after all. They were too cheap to pay for one. So they could easily have fallen . . ."

"Into the mixer?"

"Yes."

"And what would have happened then, Fergal, if they had fallen into the mixer?"

Fergal looked at her across the table.

"You know, Charlotte," he said. "You know . . . you know perfectly well what was at the other end of the production line."

"Cans?"

"Yes, cans."

"Mr. and Mrs. Dimble-Smith?"

"Yes."

"In cans?"

"Hmm."

The dessert menus arrived. There was a protracted silence as they studied them. Then Fergal spoke. "Do you think we should suggest it?" he said.

"To who?"

"The police."

"That they do what?"

"Open up a few of the cans."

Charlotte looked at him. She shook her head firmly. "No, Fergal," she said. "We've no proof. It's only a theory. And anyway, they'd never believe us."

"Why not?"

Charlotte sighed. "Because we're only children, remember. They never do believe you, Fergal, when you're just a child. And we could be wrong. Maybe they escaped and got away."

"Well, I hope I never see them again."

"Me too."

"Not in the flesh or in a . . ."

"Or what, Fergal? Or see them in a what?"

"Nothing, Charlotte. Nothing."

Charlotte's father leaned over toward them. "Well, you two, have you decided on your desserts?"

"Ice cream for me, I think," Charlotte said.

"Same here," Fergal said. "Two scoops, please."

The waiter returned to take their orders. Fergal's mother hadn't quite decided. She was dithering between the banoffee pie and the peach melba.

"Your peach melba," she asked the waiter. "Is it made with fresh peaches? Or are they from a can?"

"Fresh, of course, madam!" the waiter said, somewhat indignantly. "We only use the finest and the freshest ingredients here."

"Good. I'll have the peach melba then. I just wanted to check. I wouldn't have had it if it was out of a can."

"Very wise, madam," the waiter said. "Very wise."

He went off with their orders.

"I think," Fergal said to Charlotte, as they sat waiting for their desserts to arrive, "that as I'm going to have some time on my hands, now that I've stopped collecting cans, and as jars aren't very interesting, that I might take up ice skating."

"Ice skating?"

"I could do it on a Saturday morning, instead of going to the supermarket. Would you like to try it?"

"Yes, I've always fancied ice skating myself," Charlotte said. "Do you think it's a lot of fun?"

"Probably," Fergal said.

"Do you think . . . you have adventures?"

Fergal looked doubtful. But then his face broke into a smile.

"Possibly," he said. "That is . . . you never know, do you? You never know what might turn up."

"No," Charlotte agreed, "you don't."

At which point their ice cream turned up. Along with Mrs. Bamfield's peach melba. She was pleased to note that the peaches were, as the waiter had promised, perfectly fresh.

They weren't canned. Not like some peaches. Or certain other things. Best left unmentioned. In cans best left unopened. In places best left undisturbed. That was the way cans were, really, especially cans without labels. You never really knew what you were going to get until you opened them. They were a little bit like life itself — you never knew what it might contain or have in store. No, you couldn't be sure about cans at all. And the odd thing was, that even when a can — or a life — seemed quite, quite empty and devoid of promise . . .

It could still be full to the very brim.

Of rather extraordinary . . .

Surprises.

FOOTNOTE

The Dimble-Smiths' factory was closed down, the machinery was dismantled, and the buildings eventually demolished. The many cans, both full and empty, were taken away by a private clearance company to be disposed of at the local tip.

They didn't get that far, however, as the man taking them away, one Chester Hagget, a man with an eye for a bargain and a magpie-like attraction to anything silver and shiny, decided that there was a little extra money to be made here and that he was just the chap to make it.

So he drove all the cans home to his small holding in the country, where he dumped them in the yard and sorted out the full ones from the empty.

The empty ones he put in the shed, in the belief that they would "come in handy one day." As for the full ones, knowing them to contain pet food, he made a short phone call to an acquaintance of his.

"Sogger?" he said. "Is that you?"

"What if it is?" Sogger answered. "Who wants to know?"

"It's me. Chester."

Sogger's tone changed. He'd been worried that perhaps it was the police, or possibly the local Trading Standards Authority.

"So what can I do for you, boy?"

"Your market stall," Hagget said.

"What about it?"

"You sell pet food on it?"

"I sell everything," Sogger said. "Why?"

"I've got a good deal on pet food for you here," Hagget told him. "Got a big load of cans of it, going cheap. Only thing is, they've got no labels. So you'd need to get a few run off and stick them on yourself. But I'll give you a good price as allowance for the inconvenience."

After some haggling, a deal was struck. Sogger came round to collect the cans.

One tin was opened as a sample of merchandise.

"Bit whiffy," Sogger said, his nose turning up.

"Well, you don't have to eat it," Hagget reminded him. "It's for pets."

"What pets, exactly?" Sogger said. "Dogs or cats?"

"Both or either," Hagget told him. "I shouldn't think they'll be fussy. I don't think dogs go refusing to eat what's in a can 'cause the label says it's for cats. Nor cats neither."

"True," Sogger agreed. He took a wad of notes out, held together with a rubber band. "Cash suit you?" he said.

"Better than anything." Hagget nodded. "My favorite."

So the deal was done and the cans were loaded into Sogger's van. Just before he drove off, as he sat in the cab of the van with his elbow on the window, he leaned out and said, "I think I'll get half the labels printed up as dog food, and half as cat." He added, "I was considering getting a few printed as 'Quality Beef and Brisket,' but that might be pushing things too far."

"Could be risky," Hagget agreed. "Don't want to go poisoning anyone."

He banged farewell on the van, and Sogger drove off.

Sogger did as he said he would. He ran the labels off himself on his home computer and got Mrs. Sogger to stick them all on the cans. Then he put the cans on display, a few dozen at a time, on his market stall wherever he set it up, or he sold them from the back of his van at flea markets.

BEST QUALITY DOG AND CAT FOOD, his display card read. SPECIAL OFFER — 3-4-2.

Fergal's father happened to be at the local flea market one Sunday morning. He was trying to get rid of his old golf clubs, but so far he had had no takers. But finally he got an acceptable offer for them, and his business concluded, he went to wander around and see what others had to sell.

Best quality dog and cat food.

At bargain prices too.

He bought a few cans to take home to Angus. The cat deserved an occasional treat.

"Got some cat food for Angus," Mr. Bamfield announced when he returned home. "It was on special at the flea market."

Mrs. Bamfield looked at the three cans of cat food dubiously.

"Did you get me a present too?" she asked.

"Why would you want cat food?" Mr. Bamfield asked.

Mrs. Bamfield didn't speak to him for the rest of the afternoon, which she spent out in the garden uprooting weeds.

Fergal had gone to the cinema that day, with Charlotte and a couple of other friends. Fergal seemed to be a whole lot more popular recently, after the press coverage of his escapades with the cans.

While Mr. Bamfield was making a cup of tea, Angus came in from outside and rubbed himself against his leg, meowing for something to eat.

"Okay, Angus." Mr. Bamfield smiled. "I know. You're hungry."

He took a tin of the new cat food from the cupboard and got the opener. He opened the can and shook the contents out into Angus's bowl, as the cat meowed impatiently.

Mr. Bamfield went to mash the food up with the special fork reserved for Angus.

That was when he noticed something. In there among the food, lying there in the bowl.

He fished it out and inspected it. It was a nail.

A great big toenail.

How on earth did that ever get in there? Mr. Bamfield wondered. Wasn't that the strangest — not to say most revolting — thing? A toenail. In a can of pet food. Just fancy that. And the nail looked like a human one too. He couldn't possibly give this food to the cat now. Mr. Bamfield scraped the food into the bin and dished up some sardines for Angus instead. Plainly a bit dodgy, that cheap flea-market stuff. He really shouldn't have bought it. He dropped the cans into the bin.

Good job he'd noticed that big sharp toenail though, Mr. Bamfield thought. The cat could have choked on it.

It was highly dangerous, something like that.

It really was.

It could easily have proved fatal.